SNEAK PEEK:

Rage of Babylon

Smashed Dreams Series

CONTENTS

Sneak Peek One

The fanfare cries lingered long and loud, accentuating feelings of majestic nobility that permeated the royal architectural walls of Babylon.

"Ouch! You pricked me, you idiot!" bellowed Nebuchadnezzar.

"Sorry Sire," Amukkan stammered.

King Nebuchadnezzar rolled his eyes as his personal attendant bowed low, so low that he almost fell over.

"When are you going to stop tripping over your own feet?" Nebuchadnezzar snarled rudely.

Amukkan was a bit off-balance today. He was shaky, more so than usual. However, he continued his usual chattering.

"Sire, did you know that the chickens that are to be slaughtered for the feast of the New Year's Festival aren't slaughtered as yet?"

"Maybe if you worried more about your own job rather than the cooks' food, you wouldn't prick me so much," growled Nebuchadnezzar through gritted teeth.

"Lift your arm please, Sire," Amukkan beckoned, ignoring Nebuchadnezzar's last comment.

Amukkan was a small man with a cheeky smile and long, thin, bony fingers. He was King Nebuchadnezzar's personal attendant, who could be found chattering alongside Nebuchadnezzar about everything that went on in the palace.

Most days, Nebuchadnezzar grew weary of him – however, Amukkan's gossip was the king's way of keeping up with what was going on behind the scenes in the palace. He lifted both arms higher. He was a large man. Actually, he was *very* large, with a round middle. He was also very loud. Known for his hot temper, he was a dreadful man who struck fear in everyone. In fact, one could hear him coming from a mile away, but no one dared to challenge him for he was known to be impractical, unreasonable, and even insane. These words described King Nebuchadnezzar perfectly.

"Now for the oil," said Amukkan, removing the cover from the flask of oil he had recovered from the nearby table. He poured a generous amount before covering his hands in the thick, greasy goo. "Kneel please, Your Highness," he said.

Nebuchadnezzar kneeled and bowed his head. He allowed Amukkan to rub the oil onto his bald head.

"Your war tattoos are magnificent, Your Majesty," Amukkan said with admiration. He oiled the inked images that were tattooed from front to back of the king's head.

"Each a mark for each victory—a sacred engraftment for every win," Nebuchadnezzar bragged.

"You know, I've heard the army whispering," said Amukkan in a low voice.

"Oh?" said Nebuchadnezzar. "What do they say?" he asked.

"They wonder why it is only the king and war generals who bear such tattoos," he said, as he slowly moved his hands down and began to rub the oil into the king's beard.

"Everyone wants a mark of honor," snarled Nebuchadnezzar. "No one wants to submit to years of loyalty and hard work." He chuckled. "You have to work to achieve a mark. It takes hard work and lots of women and wine to carry you through." He took the goblet of wine from the temple slave boy.

Amukkan waited while the king took a long drink.

"Ah! Excellent wine," said Nebuchadnezzar. "This is why I love conquering countries. The moment I conquer a country, whatever they own belongs to me."

"Yes, Your Majesty," said Amukkan, as he finished applying oil to the king's beard.

Nebuchadnezzar's beard was adorned in gold and precious jewels. It reached just above his knees. What a frightful sight was he—dreadful to be around and dreadful to behold. Nebuchadnezzar usually said that his beard gave him the answers to certain problems. He was very proud of it, and from time to time during a conversation or when deep in thought, he would stroke it.

Nebuchadnezzar reached for the golden goblet again. He drank deeply. The dark red liquid stained his lips. "This wine is rich and memorable," Nebuchadnezzar said, bringing the goblet to his mouth again. After taking several gulps, he let out a loud sigh.

Amukkan helped him to his feet. Then he raised both arms again. Amukkan draped the bright, blood-red ceremonial robes around him. If all went well and the gods were happy, they would, led by the king, take part in a procession from his temple to the New Year's House located outside the city walls.

The citizens of Babylon would line the streets, either very somber or excited, depending on the fate the gods Marduk and Nabu had dished out.

"Ah, Res Sattim. We begin another year," sighed Nebuchadnezzar, taking another long gulp.

"Maybe Marduk and Nabu will smile upon us and send us good crops this year," said Amukkan.

"Maybe Marduk and the crown prince Nabu will send me more lands to conquer so that I may take their crops and livestock and gain even more power," growled Nebuchadnezzar, patting his over-large middle. He belched loudly and stretched his arms horizontally, allowing Amukkan to continue to drape the robe around him.

"This yearly ritual wearies me," he grunted. "Imagine having to kill a bull who is charging at you at top speed simply because his bowels possess a message from the gods themselves, a message of the future." He gulped the rich wine again, this time emptying his goblet.

"I'll never understand how the high priest wades through all that blood and guts."

He held his goblet away from him and squinted at it.

"I'll need a lot more wine to be able to stomach the slop." He motioned for the slave boy to fill his empty goblet.

"You're having more wine, Sire?" Amukkan's question dripped with sarcasm. "Too much wine causes one to miss his target."

"I am the king! I never miss my mark!" shouted Nebuchadnezzar. "You had better mind your tongue before I have it cut out of your head and fed to the birds!"

Amukkan, who had fallen to the floor in fear, squeaked out an apology just as the trumpets blared. "We must hurry," he mumbled, trying to regain his composure. He stumbled a bit as he reached for the fourteen-karat, solid-gold belt that was to be placed around the king's over-large middle.

"WE?" Nebuchadnezzar bellowed. "YOU must hurry!" he corrected Amukkan loudly, pronouncing each syllable as if Amukkan were a child.

Amukkan struggled to tie the belt as Nebuchadnezzar spoke. He pulled fiercely at it, yanking the back of the belt towards himself.

Nebuchadnezzar's eyes bulged. "The first trumpet is a sign that the bull is near. If I am not ready before the second trumpet," he wheezed as if out of oxygen, "I will personally see to it that you are fed to the lions!" He held his middle as if in pain.

"All done," said Amukkan, more relieved than proud. He quickly handed the king the ceremonial sword just before the second trumpet sounded. Amukkan led Nebuchadnezzar to the temple's entrance just as the second trumpet resounded. Nebuchadnezzar lined himself up in front of the gods, Marduk and Nabu. Behind Marduk and Nabu stood the high priest, dressed in white. Slaves heaved as they pushed the entrance doors open. Amukkan gasped as the bull snorted, and bellowed as he charged towards Nebuchadnezzar, who stood calmly at the entrance of the King's Temple. "For Marduk!" he suddenly shouted. Raising the ceremonial sword high above his head, he charged forward, matching the bull's speed.

Slowly, Nebuchadnezzar brought his hand down, lining the outstretched sword up with the bull's head as he ran toward it. The bull charged straight into the sword. Down came the sword, down came Nebuchadnezzar and down came the bull!

"They said I had too much wine!" Nebuchadnezzar mocked. "I got the stupid beast right through his brain!" he chuckled loudly as applause and laughter went up through the crowds. He looked down at the animal that now lay dead at his feet. "Just look at the monster, thick and meaty as can be," he grunted. "If he brings good news, he'll make a fine centerpiece for the feast tonight."

"For Marduk!" he yelled as he thrust his sword into the air.

"For Marduk!" the crowds shouted in return.

Sneak Peek Two

There was war in the skies as the thunder growled and snarled at the lightning that danced playfully across the sky. The clouds opened their bowels, releasing torrents of rain that beat down relentlessly on Babylon. A loud crash, followed by a wail, resounded from the depths of the temple, deep within the king's bedchambers.

Nebuchadnezzar brought a shaking hand to his head. The impact of the cold hard floor that had collided with his head left a throbbing, excruciating pain that was intensifying by the second. Thunder continued to rumble and shadows danced across the bedchamber, giving birth to a petrifying, creepy atmosphere. Nebuchadnezzar shuddered as the entrance doors to the bedchamber opened. He closed his eyes in dread.

"Sire?" That was Arioch's voice. "Are you okay, Sire?"

Slowly, Nebuchadnezzar opened his eyes. Standing over him was Arioch, the first advisor to the king, war general and battle strategist. Arioch was tall and muscular. His bald head was covered in tattoos, and his tanned skin was rugged and rough, having suffered years of war. A patch of animal skin covered his right eye. He had lost this eye in one of the greatest battles of all time. Arioch, who was a very skilled swordsman, had led many of Nebuchadnezzar's troops into battle. Nebuchadnezzar had great respect for him, and many a decision was given to him, which he carried out at appointed times.

"OH!" Nebuchadnezzar wailed loudly, holding his head in despair. His bloodshot eyes were filled with tears, and every inch of his body glistened with sweat. He shivered and trembled with a fear none had ever witnessed in him. "Is my gold okay?" Suddenly, he sat up intending to examine the room.

"No, Sire!" said Arioch, kneeling beside him. "You must be still until the healer arrives." He motioned to Amukkan. "Bring some valerian at once!" Arioch commanded. "We need to calm his nerves."

Amukkan hurried away in swift obedience. "The healer will be here soon, my king," Arioch assured him.

"Healer!" exclaimed Nebuchadnezzar. "I don't need a healer!" he continued, fluttering his hands in front of his face as if he could not be bothered with such a thought. Droplets of sweat continued to furiously trickle down his brow. "Bring the royal sorcerers and magicians to me," he commanded in an almost steady voice.

"Sire, surely brewing up a nice herbal remedy is far better than conjuring up..." Arioch's voice trailed off.

Nebuchadnezzar held up the first steady hand of the night. "Bring every sorcerer, magician, fortune-teller, and enchanter to me," he ordered through clenched teeth. He shoved aside the valerian Amukkan offered him, and said, "I have a dream I need to be interpreted."

Arioch nodded with understanding. "Right away, Sire!"

SNEAK PEEK THREE

An earsplitting silence fell over the throne room. The thunderous hush, rising from the depths of the chambers of the royal court, surrounded Daniel, enclosing him in its firm grip. Filled with confidence, his heart remained prayerful. "Dear Lord, walk with me," he silently prayed. The journey to the throne was before him. He had to stand before a bad-tempered king.

Remembering to keep his eyes lowered, he slowly made his way towards the throne. Step by step, he placed one foot in front of the other, progressing towards the goal, towards Nebuchadnezzar, towards the insane king.

The room started to spin as Arioch announced his presence, and the unfolding of each event seemed to slip by as if they were a part of a fleeting dream. "Speak through me my Lord," he prayed silently.

"You don't look like a sorcerer!" Nebuchadnezzar snarled. Nebuchadnezzar's eyes sliced over Daniel. "Is it true that you can tell me exactly what I dreamt?" He leaned forward, a glimmer of hope in his eyes. Raising his head, Daniel looked the king of Babylon in the eye for the very first time. A dreadful sight was he. His bloodshot eyes were surrounded by purple shadows from lack of sleep. His beard was a tangled mess. He must not have taken food or water for days for his lips were dry and cracked with dehydration. His stony stare bore through Daniel. "Does he speak?" Nebuchadnezzar asked. The court launched into laughter. "What do they call you?" asked Nebuchadnezzar.

"Your Highness, I am Daniel." Daniel approached and stood before the king.

"You do not bow to your king?" Nebuchadnezzar growled.

"I bow to the one and only Lord God Almighty, The Creator, King of kings and Lord of lords, who is the Revealer of all mysteries," said Daniel.

"How dare you! You stand before me claiming the majesty and greatness of another king?" Nebuchadnezzar was fuming. He began to get to his feet but sank back onto his throne, weak from the effort.

"It is he who will first tell you what you dreamt, and then he will tell you the meaning of your dream," Daniel declared quietly.

"Well then, where is he?" exclaimedNebuchadnezzar, looking around hopeful.

"Is he made of gold or silver? A King of kings should be made of pure diamond!" laughed Amukkan.

"Silence!" Nebuchadnezzar shouted, looking annoyed. "Did you bring him?" Nebuchadnezzar asked, almost desperately.

"My God is already here. He is everywhere," exclaimed Daniel. He looked over at Shadrach, Meshach and Abednego, who stood with their heads bowed. Their lips moved silently. The entire throne room burst into laughter, except for Shadrach, Meshach, and Abednego. "No wise man, enchanter, fortune-teller, sorcerer or magician can tell you your dream, Sire," he continued, firmly confident that he was right.

"I'm told that you can help me," Nebuchadnezzar said quietly.

"*I* cannot help you! However, there is a God in heaven who can reveal all mysteries," said Daniel. "He has shown you what will happen in the days to come."

Nebuchadnezzar shuddered. "Continue," he said.

"As Your Majesty was lying there, your mind turned to things to come, and the Revealer of mysteries showed you what is going to happen in the future. As for me, this mystery has been revealed to me, not because I have greater wisdom than anyone else alive, but so that Your Majesty may know the interpretation and understand exactly what it is that went through your mind. Your Majesty looked, and there before you stood a very tall statue—an enormous, dazzling statue, awesome in appearance."

King Nebuchadnezzar's eyes widened.

"The head of the statue was made of pure gold, its chest and arms of silver, its belly, and thighs of bronze, its legs of iron, and its feet were made partly of iron and partly of baked clay. While you were watching, a rock was cut out of a mountain, but not by human hands. It struck the statue on its feet of iron and clay and smashed them. Then the iron, the clay, the bronze, the silver, and the gold were all broken in pieces and became like chaff on a threshing floor in the summer. The winds swept them away without leaving a trace. But the rock that struck the statue became a huge mountain that filled the whole earth."

Nebuchadnezzar's widened eyes were fixed on Daniel as he spoke. The throne room that had once launched into boisterous laughter was now silent.

"This was the dream, and now we will interpret it for the king." He took a deep breath. "Your Majesty, you are the king of kings. The God of heaven has given you dominion, power, might, and glory; in your hands, he has placed all mankind, including the beasts of the field and the birds of the sky. Wherever they live, he has made you ruler over them all. You are that head of gold.

Nebuchadnezzar was awestruck. He could hardly believe what he was hearing!

Daniel continued. "After you, another kingdom will arise and reign, a kingdom of silver that will be inferior to yours. Next, a third kingdom, one of bronze, will rule over the whole earth. Finally, there will be a fourth kingdom, strong as iron—for iron can break and smash everything in its path—and as iron breaks things into small pieces, so it will crush and break all the others before it. Then another kingdom will arise, made partly of baked clay and partly of iron. It will be a divided kingdom; yet it will have some of the strength of the kingdom of iron in it, even as you saw the iron mixed with the clay. As the toes were partly iron and partly clay, so too, this kingdom will be partly strong and partly brittle. And just as you saw the iron mixed with baked clay, so too the kings and people will be a mixed, but very strong group, but they will not remain united, any more than iron when it is mixed with clay."

He paused for a brief moment and then said, "In the time of those kings, the God of heaven will set up a kingdom that will never be destroyed, nor will it be left in the hands of human beings. It will crush all those kingdoms and bring them to an end, but it will itself endure forever. This is the meaning of the vision of the rock being cut out of a mountain, but not by human hands— a rock that broke the iron, the clay, the bronze, the silver, and the gold in pieces. The great God of the universe has shown the king what will take place in the future. The dream is true, and its interpretation is trustworthy."

Nebuchadnezzar rose to his feet and fell prostrate before Daniel. "Surely your God is the Lord of gods and the Revealer of all mysteries for He has revealed this great mystery to me." Then he signaled to Arioch. "Daniel, I name you governor over the entire province of Babylon. I present to you a royal chariot, a ruby ring and royal silk robes."

Daniel's eyes widened as the ring was placed on his finger. He could not speak, but silently, he thanked the God of heaven for His loving favor upon him.

Then Nebuchadnezzar proclaimed, "I also place you in charge of all of the wise men in Babylon, for your God is truly the source of all wisdom."

CHOSEN

"SILENT SOLDIER SERIES"

This book is a work of fiction with close reference, as much as possible, to the biblical story of Esther found in The Holy Bible. Names, characters, places, and incidents are a product of the author's imagination or are used fictitiously. Any resemblance to actual persons, living or dead, business establishments, events or locales is entirely coincidental.

Chosen

"Silent Soldier Series"

Copyright © 2016 by Elaine E Thompson

Dedication

To Daddy, Mommy, Chase, and Darrell with love

PROLOGUE

The city lay swollen with revenge, defeat pouring from its veins. The smell of death was everywhere. Armed soldiers crawled in and out of dark corridors and crevices like maggots, proclaiming triumph over death's prizes. Death's vengeance was evident, and the stench of the rotting city as it lay deteriorating choked Mordecai to tears––or maybe it was the smoke that permeated the air, reducing the supply of oxygen that once saturated Babylon's once clean atmosphere. He peeped from behind the half-burnt structure that was once his home.

The trauma of warfare had devastated Babylon. Cyrus, Emperor of Persia, had ordered the capture of the city and its citizens. Babylon, which once stood as an impenetrable fortress surrounded by thick walls, towers, and moats, had been burned to the ground. The city's ashes were smoking like those of a raging wildfire.

The city's moats, a line of defense implemented by King Nebuchadnezzar, that once protected the city from any unwanted company, now lay dry and waterless, exposing Babylon to thousands of Persian and Median soldiers. Cyrus had diverted the Euphrates River, preventing it from flowing into the city's moats. This allowed Medo-Persian guards and military full access to the city of Babylon.

Mordecai leaned carefully against the hot structure, the only cover from the hundreds of guards who seemed to be everywhere. His stomach growled loudly. He had spent the last hour praying to God to provide food for him and his family. It seemed that between starvation and a sword's blade, death was inevitable for Mordecai and his family.

During the siege, most Babylonians feasted upon leather sandals. It was a meal that would trick the stomach into survival mode and gave the destitute the chance to live at least one more day. It had been a rough four years. All meat was scarce because hunting was forbidden. The Babylonians ate pot-cakes during the siege. They were a mixed breed, wild dogs that fed on rubbish and filth for survival. The meat was stringy and was only eaten out of desperation because deer, antelope, and venison were out of the question for Babylonians in hiding.

Mordecai was a Jew who did not resort to desperate acts. By law, Jews did not eat unclean foods. The Law of Moses and its preservation was vital to the Jews. The Law was their lifeline for it was through them that God would send a Savior. It was through them that God would redeem the world. They had been chosen to be the medium through which a divine King would come; and not just any king, but the Redeemer of the world who would pay the price for humanity's sins that were committed from the beginning of time since the very first humans, Adam and Eve.

"Just a small amount of milk, Lord," Mordecai prayed silently, "if only for Hadassah." Mordecai looked around sadly. Farms and wheat fields had been burned beyond recognition, and the land was patrolled three times a day. Just as two soldiers, armed with swords, hurried by, Mordecai's attention was caught by a slight movement. He squinted curiously at the burnt structure across the way. "There it is again!" he thought to himself. He looked wildly about him and then squinted again. His heart thumped vigorously. Whatever it was must have moved on, for when Mordecai looked again all was still.

"You're brave," said a voice behind him. Mordecai jumped, for right next to him stood a hooded figure. He could not make out his face. However, he could tell the man standing next to him had a beard.

"I-I..." stammered Mordecai. "Take this," he said, quickly shoving something into Mordecai's hand--and as quickly as he came, he was gone. Mordecai's eyes filled with hope as soon as he saw the unleavened bread and the skin filled with goat's milk. His heart sang out in gratitude as his right hand enclosed around the chunk of bread and water skin. A piece of unleavened bread was the perfect meal for Hadassah. "Thank you, Lord," Mordecai smiled as he gave thanks to God for answering his prayer so quickly.

Slowly, he made his way back to where his family was hiding. Two more soldiers passed by. Just a few feet farther and soon he would be inside what was once his home. All was still. Careful to look around first, he ducked inside the deconstructed doorway of the wooden structure.

"Who goes there?" a gruff voice said from within.

Mordecai's heart sank. He stuffed the bread and water skin inside the inner piece of his robe.

"Show yourself this instant!" the guard shouted.

Slowly Mordecai straightened up as he raised his hands.

"What do you think you're doing?" the guard growled at him.

"B-b-b..." Mordecai stammered, shaking uncontrollably.

"Morde!" a tiny voice cried out. A tiny girl with waist-length black hair and heavy eyelashes waddled over to him, fastening herself to his leg. Mordecai breathed a sigh of relief, but his heart sank quickly. Filled with turmoil, he looked around for his aunt and uncle.

"Who are you looking for, boy?" growled the first guard who was the larger of the two.

"There's just us now boy!" the second guard snarled. "Those two are as good as dead. They will never survive the journey." He pointed at a tiny-framed woman and a tall man who lay sprawled out on the ground of the home. They were both gaunt due to starvation. Their eyes bulged as they stared into the distance at something only they could see.

A tall, burly captain stuck his head into the structure. "The city has surrendered!" he shouted. "Round up the captives, then burn the city to the ground, and be quick about it! Take them to the ships!" the captain commanded.

Mordecai cried out as two guards heaved him onto his feet and carried him and a terrified Hadassah away. He hugged Hadassah close and vowed to protect her with his life.

Mordecai and Hadassah, along with the other citizens, poured out from the outskirts of the city. Some tried to escape, hungry for the taste of freedom and desperate to escape the wrath of their enemy. Balls of fiery hay rained down from above, matching the enemy's unforgiving demeanor, only to trap those trying to flee, and burning the lifeless city beyond recognition, leaving no hope for redemption. He cringed as screams of anguish and cries of despair rang out towards heaven as the Jewish race cried out to God for deliverance. Again, they were being led away into exile. They cried out for divine intervention. They cried out for a miracle. However, little did they know that God had long heard their cries, and the cries of their ancestors, and that this was the end of the seventy-year prophecy that God himself had fulfilled.

CHAPTER ONE

"There is none more stunning than you in all the empire, my queen," said Xerxes as he raised his chalice. "Shall we toast to your health and a long, dynamic reign?"

Vashti smiled and pressed her goblet against Xerxes' raised chalice. "I'm flattered," she purred. "May I add that there is none more remarkable than you are, my king?" She smiled sweetly at him before returning her focus to her plate of food.

"The empire is growing quickly," said Xerxes. "We make a great team," he added.

"I agree," said Vashti. This rabbit stew is very tender," she said, patting her mouth with the white cloth that had been neatly folded across her lap. "Please send my compliments to the cook," she told the servant to her right. She straightened her back and raised her chin slightly.

"So, is it true?" asked Vashti.

"Is what true?" asked Xerxes. He focused his attention on his own plate of rabbit stew.

"Is it true you're going to war with Greece?" she asked, slowly pronouncing each syllable.

"Word sure travels quickly, even without an official royal declaration. Maybe I should get rid of my royal messengers and have *gossip* do the job for me," said Xerxes as he spooned up some of the food and brought it to his lips. He paused, his spoon mid-air. "Who told you?"

Vashti lowered her eyes. "I heard my handmaidens whispering."

Xerxes swallowed some of the rabbit stew then chuckled. "Are they handmaidens or spies?"

"You could have told me," said Vashti. It was evident she was trying not to raise her voice. "I'm the queen, for crying out loud!"

Xerxes laughed. "I don't need the queen's permission to go to war."

"Just a moment ago you were saying what a great team we make," she pointed out sarcastically.

"Does the notion of queen confuse you after all of these years, my Darling?" asked Xerxes. He signaled to his wine bearer for more wine.

Vashti sat and stared coolly at him.

Xerxes brought his face closer to hers. "A queen supports her king no matter what," he said, in a low, dangerous voice.

"War brings pain and suffering! What about all of those women and children?" she exclaimed. "War is not the answer. There are other ways Xerxes!"

"Enlighten me, my queen," said Xerxes.

"Marriage is one way," replied Vashti.

"Who's hand will we trade Vashti?" he said, his voice rising with each syllable. "You failed to give me little princes and princesses."

Vashti's face reddened. "You always knew where to hurt me."

"I did not mean to hurt you," Xerxes replied. "It's just together we stand but divided we fall. You cannot be against me Vashti. We are one."

"The damage is already done." Vashti brought her goblet slowly to her lips. She paused, her goblet midair. "I have not given you little prince and princesses *yet*. They will come when the gods smile upon us." She drank slowly then squinted at him. "A war will not make the gods smile upon us. A war brings much bloodshed..."

"War is war! I know what it brings!" Xerxes interrupted, raising his voice. "I will do whatever it takes to uphold this dynasty, and that includes war." He took a long drink of wine from his chalice. "You want the rebels to go unpunished? Do you want to remain queen? Or do you prefer to see those who rebel against us on the throne while we take up residence in their dungeons because of a little bloodshed?"

"Maybe you will do a lot better in the dungeons than I will, as long as you have your chalice to keep you company," she spat cruelly.

Xerxes reached forward in a single move and smacked her face.

She gasped in surprise.

"You will mind your tongue when you speak to me," he snarled. "I am the king," he said, pronouncing each syllable. "Or have you forgotten?" he asked in a low, dangerous voice.

Vashti's lip quivered, and tears poured down her face as she got up and ran out of the large dining hall.

Xerxes pushed his rabbit stew around his plate. He was no longer hungry. He had wounded Vashti's pride. This was evident. He made a mental note to pay her a visit later when things had blown over. The doors to the great dining hall suddenly opened and in hurried Megabyzus.

"Your highness!" he said breathlessly. "You're needed in the kitchens!"

Xerxes got to his feet and hastily followed Megabyzus out of the dining hall and into the kitchens. "What is it?" he asked grimly. The look on Megabyzus' face had told him that something had gone wrong.

"It's Thomas, the royal food taster." He pointed to a chubby, oversized man who now lay on the floor toppled and frail in a heap. He held his abdomen, his face crumpled in pain. "We have already fetched the doctor."

"How do you feel, Your Highness?" Megabyzus asked.

"I feel fine," said Xerxes. He knelt beside the man who lay balled up in pain. "Check on the queen. Take her to safety until we get to the bottom of this," he commanded. "What was the last thing he tasted?" he asked.

"Strawberry pudding," replied one of the servants. "It was to be served next, Your Grace."

"Bring it forth at once," commanded Megabyzus.

"It seemed a bit sandy," Thomas moaned. "I continued to eat as my job commands." He began to vomit profusely.

"Megabyzus dipped his fingers into the soft mixture and rubbed his fingers together. "It is rather sandy."

Thomas vomited again, this time, blood. He coughed copiously then vomited again.

"After the cook made the meal whose hands did the food pass through?" asked Xerxes.

"Mine," said a young servant girl who started to tremble. Her voice quavered with fear. "After the cook made the pudding, Thomas tasted it, and it was to be taken out to your grace. I had forgotten to garnish it because Artanos had distracted me. So, I went to find the chopped mint. I placed the chopped mint on top and asked Thomas to taste it again. That is when Thomas..." her voice trailed.

"Find Artanos and seize him!" Xerxes commanded the surrounding soldiers. They hastily obeyed his bidding.

"Is that the truth, child?" Megabyzus asked.

She nodded; her eyes welled over with tears.

"Then you have nothing to fear," Xerxes assured her. "Where is Artanos?"

"He left the moment I brought Thomas over to taste the food again," the servant girl said.

Just then, the doctor entered the kitchens and knelt beside Thomas.

Thomas moaned again before vomiting more blood. His breath was shallow and coming faster by the second.

"What is it, doctor?" Xerxes asked.

"There is no sign of poison, for poison reddens the eyes." He squinted at Thomas. "We will know soon enough," he said as he knitted his eyebrows and felt the back of Thomas' throat. Thomas gagged before vomiting again. "Can I examine what Thomas has eaten?" asked the doctor as he felt Thomas' pulse.

Megabyzus brought the small dish of strawberry pudding to him.

"Here is Artanos" reported a soldier. He shoved a bewildered and trembling Artanos to the ground.

"It seems to be crushed glass, Your Grace," said the doctor.

"There was volcanic glass on his cot when we retrieved him from his quarters, Your Highness," said one of the soldiers.

"Take Thomas to the infirmary. Do everything you can for him, doctor!" commanded Xerxes. He looked down at Artanos his eyes filled with anger. "Take Artanos to the dungeons. There he will await trial for high treason!"

CHAPTER TWO

"Feels like I'm always eating," laughed Mordecai as he sat back in his chair and patted his middle. He was a short, plump man with a round middle. He was a stout middle-aged fellow who had adopted his orphan cousin, Hadassah a few years back. Her parents had both died during the attack on Babylon. It had been a miracle that Hadassah had survived. He had taken her under his wings, and since then, the bond between them was unbreakable.

Mordecai and Hadassah were both Jews. However, Hadassah looked far from Jewish. In fact, the most Jewish thing about her was her name, Hadassah. Jews tended to have lighter color hair were usually of medium height, and heavily tanned. Their beliefs did not allow them to eat certain foods and so fish and raw vegetables made up most of their diet, although a goat or sheep was an occasional prized treat.

Mordecai was the palace's book-keeper—he was one of its verification officers. He reviewed the stone tablets daily to ensure that the budget was being adhered to in the palace. Though meager, in terms of means, their lives were strangely comfortable.

Hadassah smiled at him. "You eat three much-needed meals a day, cousin," she assured him. "Your meals are just memorable, that's all," she teased.

"I would imagine if they are anything like this one, then they are beyond memorable," chimed As-Ho. "We could use a cook like you where I come from. My mother is obsessed with the traditional way of food preparation." He sighed heavily before pointing to his meal. "I've never known frumenty to be so sweet and delicious. It's usually prepared as a savory meal. However, I feel a meal of this texture *needs* to be sweet and loaded with cinnamon, sugar, and honey. It is more welcoming to the palate, especially on an early morning like this one. This is outstanding, Hadassah!"

Hadassah smiled. "Thank you," she said politely.

As-Ho nodded.

"I'm glad you are enjoying your meal," said Mordecai. "May I add that it is refreshing to be in the company of another who loves the Lord?"

"Thank you, Mordecai. It is an honor to be here." He smiled at Hadassah, who quickly looked down at her plate with a sudden exaggerated interest in adding more honey to the frumenty she was eating.

"I'm sure Hadassah here would love to hear all about your journey. Wouldn't you, Hadassah?" Mordecai nudged.

Hadassah gave As-Ho another polite smile before adding more honey to her meal. She nodded, fighting the urge to send a glare in Mordecai's direction.

"Well, my journey through Egypt was more humid than expected, but despite this, I was able to water my camels every two days. At times there were sandstorms for miles, but we pushed through. It was a rather long and hard journey, but well worth it," he chuckled as he beamed at Hadassah.

She looked down at her plate.

"Did you hear the king is raising taxes again?" Mordecai interrupted. "Twelve percent of food, crop and cattle will be paid to the crown monthly."

"So, I gathered from the declaration sent out throughout the empire," As-Ho said as he chugged down the water from the silver goblet that matched his bowl. "You manage the budget of the royal treasury. Must the king force such high taxation on us?"

"I am not at liberty to discuss the treasury's affairs. However, I will say this. No matter what is done to us, we will survive if we put our complete dependence on the Lord. He brought us out of Babylon. He allowed Cyrus to give the order for our people to rebuild the wall of our homeland. What is a little tax going to do to us?"

"Can your residence handle such high demand in tax?" As-Ho asked curiously.

"We will manage," interrupted Hadassah. This had been the most she had said to As-Ho since he had shown up in Hunting Valley declaring his love for her. There was no denying her beauty. She was tall and slender, with a graceful figure that was somewhat more than her fair share.

"This new taxation doesn't frighten me," he boasted. "I've never felt more secure since our people were herded out of Babylon like cattle." He coughed as he chugged down more water. "My domicile sells livestock and cattle to the castle of Prince Namur, Satrap of Egypt. Business is good," he bragged. "Everyone is happy. My sisters spin thread for extra money. We have many servants so you would have plenty of help, Hadassah."

Hadassah looked over at the golden Egyptian comb that still lay on the table where he had presented it to her. It was beautiful, and one of a kind. Small rubies lined the edges. He must have spent a fortune on it. Still, she cringed at the thought of being married to him.

"You know I always said I would never do the traditional mohar and mattan. I'm not a gold and silver kind of guy." He laughed nervously. "My mohar would be paid in jewels, and my mattan would be gifts of cattle and livestock and even servants, which may I add, I think you would make good use of around here. I will pay you well for little Hadassah here."

"Marriage is not the solution for a higher tax," said Hadassah bluntly.

"With war on the horizon and the king's taxes rising so rapidly, I would say joining domiciles is the perfect solution," said As-Ho as he gulped down more water. "We Jews need to stick together. It is the only way to survive the struggles that lie ahead." He fluttered his hands in front of his face as if he could not be bothered to speak about it anymore. "Let's not squabble about it now. You know what I am saying is quite true."

"Excuse me. I need to get more honey," replied Hadassah. As she gathered her skirts and made her way to the kitchens as fast as she could, she heard Mordecai say to As-Ho,

"The Lord has taken care of Hadassah and me then, and he will most certainly take care of us now. A higher tax does not frighten either of us," said Mordecai.

Hadassah paused to take a breath. Her heart slowed as she reeled in her frustration. "Who did As-Ho think he was, showing up like that making demands of marriage?" She bustled around the kitchen as she prepared the final course of the meal.

"Why are you so discourteous to our guest?"

"I'm doing the best I can!" Hadassah said as she quickly spun around. The silverware crashed to the floor. "He's far older than I am!"

"Give him a chance. You may like him," said Mordecai as he knelt beside her and began grabbing the spoons and knives that had fallen to the floor. "Ouch!" he exclaimed.

"What is wrong?" asked Hadassah.

"The knife nicked me," he replied as a trickle of blood dribbled its way down his arm.

She led him to a nearby chair. "Hold still and don't move," Hadassah instructed. She began to rummage through a nearby cupboard. "It's somewhere around here," she mumbled.

"It's fine, Hadassah," Mordecai said.

"This aloe will heal it and prevent infection," said Hadassah. She knelt beside him and rubbed the slimy salve onto his hand.

Mordecai smiled down at her. "You are good at taking care of me. Your future husband will be blessed to have you."

"You want me to wed someone who calls me *little* Hadassah!" she replied her voice barely above a whisper.

"I want you to be happy and well taken care of," said Mordecai.

"There that should do it," she said. She removed the aloe from his hand and returned it to the cupboard.

"You should be happy, Hadassah," said Mordecai.

"Taking care of you makes me happy," said Hadassah as she reached to recover another spoon. "And I can very well take care of myself."

"You will make a good wife someday," said Mordecai.

"But not today?" asked Hadassah.

"Not today," he replied.

"Oh Mordecai!" she exclaimed as she threw her arms around him. "I love you!"

Mordecai laughed loudly.

"Now let us bid him the Lord's richest blessings and send him on his way!" she said. "If I eat any more honey, I'm going to be sick." She laughed loudly as she hooked her arm around his before heading back to the dining quarters.

BRAM, BRAM, BRAM! "Open up in the name of the king!"

Hadassah sat down as Mordecai shuffled his way to the door.

"I'm coming with you," said As-Ho. He got up and accompanied Mordecai just as Mordecai opened the door.

"Royal declaration from the palace," a soldier read from a lengthy parchment. "Each citizen of the empire is to attend and witness the trial of Artanos, son of Arto, who is being charged with treason in the highest degree. This will happen at the royal gallows at the next sunrise." He paused and cleared his throat before continuing.

"At the next sunset, there will be a royal feast celebrating his Royal Highness King Xerxes and his great and dynamic empire of one hundred and twenty-seven provinces. All citizens, rich and poor, are welcome." He pulled his armor over his face and was gone as swiftly as he had come, leaving a speechless Mordecai and As-Ho at the wide-open door.

"I guess I will be here for a little longer," said As-Ho when he got his voice back. He smiled at a clearly agitated Hadassah who looked at Mordecai with a pleading look on her face.

CHAPTER THREE

"The Persian Immortals must continue!" Xerxes said firmly. "We cannot phase them out." He squared his shoulders the way his father had taught him whenever he made a point that became a permanent decision.

"They are draining the royal treasury, Your Highness. Their training..." Memukkan replied breathlessly as he struggled to keep up with the young, vigorous king.

They were on their way to the training gymnasium to view an initiation session of The Immortals. "Memukkan, if you cut off the head of the lion, how then will the lion be able to defend itself?"

Memukkan seemed deep in thought for a moment. "It's..." he replied before Xerxes interrupted him.

"Memukkan, a lion without a head is a dead lion," Xerxes replied through gritted teeth. He slowed his pace a bit. "I want to be confident when I hoist the winged lion high and ride into battle." He looked down at Memukkan. "We have had recent uprisings in both Babylon and Egypt, and if we shrink our defenses then we'll be defeated even before the battle begins," said Xerxes, approaching a flight of stairs that spiraled downward into the gymnasium.

"Yes, Your Highness, however, if we reduce taxes and the amount of hard labor on our foreign exiles, Babylon and Egypt will be happy again," advised Memukkan as he tried to keep up with Xerxes, who was taking two steps at a time.

Xerxes stopped suddenly and, turning to face Memukkan, said through clenched teeth, "I do not bend to anyone. Foreign exiles cannot tell me what to do. I am the king!"

Memukkan blinked. "Yes, Your Highness, I understand that but..."

Xerxes stared at him intently. "Are you disputing that fact?" he asked slowly before continuing toward their destination.

"I umm...uh..." Memukkan stammered.

"Try to keep up, Memukkan. I want to speak to Megabyzus before the initiation ceremony begins," he said impatiently.

Shouting could be heard as they approached the balcony of the arena. The red and gold banners proudly displayed the winged lion, Persia's emblem. "Ah, we've walked in on a very lively training session!" Memukkan smiled with enthusiasm.

A large lion sprang towards a soldier who was surrounded by a jeering mob.

"Nine thousand, nine hundred and ninety-nine men are crying out for blood," said Xerxes. "If he is defeated, the lion will have a good dinner, but if he is not, he will become a champion who will live on in the hearts of those who witness this great day." Xerxes looked on as the soldier sneered at the large cat. The soldier danced around the animal as he teased and taunted him.

"Tell me, Memukkan, what do you admire most about the lion?"

Memukkan thought carefully before answering. "His size," he said.

Xerxes laughed. "That is a great answer, Memukkan." He patted the little man on his back.

"What about you, Your Highness?" he asked.

"It's roar! A lion can paralyze its enemy with fear even before he attacks him." He looked at Memukkan. "That's why we need the Immortals. They are *the roar* of Persia."

Memukkan looked at him in admiration. "You remind me of your father."

Megabyzus!" interrupted Xerxes as the tall, dark, muscular general approached and saluted him.

He was dressed in full armor, his face hardened by war. "Good day, Your Highness," Megabyzus replied.

Xerxes squinted against the blazing sun which beat down onto the arena. "Commander," he greeted. He nodded politely.

"Have you been cooped up too long, Your Highness?" Megabyzus joked lightheartedly.

"One can never forget the heat of battle," Xerxes exclaimed. "The scorching heat in summer, the freezing cold in winter, the stench of rotting corpses and the feel of warm, wet blood will always have a place in my heart." He laughed cheerfully. Memukkan looked as though he was going to be sick. "Lighten up," Xerxes teased him. "You get used to it. After your first kill, you tend to develop a thirst for blood." He returned his attention to Megabyzus. "What have we today?"

"We have ten thousand immortal soldiers, Your Highness. All taught and trained for one sole purpose—to defend the Crown," replied Megabyzus. "Attention!" he shouted. "Initiation continues. Soldiers, group now!" Each soldier, except for the challenged one, who continued to dance around the lion, shuffled into groups of one thousand. "Halt!" Megabyzus shouted.

Xerxes looked impressed at how well the men obeyed orders.

"Your Highness, when one soldier falls, he is instantly replaced, so that our enemies will believe that this elite company is indeed immortal. There will always be ten thousand men on the battlefield, fighting to defend the Crown."

Xerxes nodded, noticing the pride Megabyzus displayed as he described the company. "How much does it cost to maintain an infantry such as this one?" asked Xerxes, studying the Immortals carefully as the lion bared its teeth at the soldier who was being challenged.

"One thousand gold pieces per week feeds them. Three thousand gold pieces per week give us proper armor, which also includes their maintenance. Five thousand gold pieces per week render us correct and appropriate weaponry."

Xerxes took a closer look at one of the soldiers. "And what about horses and ships?" he inquired, stopping in front of one of the soldiers.

Megabyzus shifted his weight before answering. "To feed the horses requires one thousand silver pieces per week and to maintain their armor costs us two thousand silver pieces per week."

Xerxes turned to him. "What about the ships?"

Megabyzus heaved a sigh.

Memukkan finally looked pleased that his earlier point of the treasury being drained by The Immortals was being made a second time.

Xerxes looked at Megabyzus, a slight sadness enveloping him. He knew that Megabyzus loved his job. However, he needed to know the budgetary needs of the company, down to the bronze pieces, to make the best decision for his empire. "I know you love this company, Megabyzus. However, I need you, to be honest with me," Xerxes assured him.

"To maintain the ships, Your Highness,will cost us ten thousand gold pieces per week. Rope, chains, anchors, paint for the sails, laborers, the captains, all incur a significant cost."

Xerxes took a deep breath. "Thank you," he said. "The Immortals are also comprised of ten thousand five-year-olds in training. Am I correct?"

Megabyzus nodded. "We also have ten thousand replacement Immortals in training."

The fighting soldier wheeled his sagaris skillfully. The lion roared loudly as the soldier nicked him with the sharp ax.

Xerxes nodded. "We need to find ways to cut costs." He turned to Memukkan. "Find a large plot of vacant land in the gardens to grow food dedicated specifically for the Immortals. No more purchasing food. Order the citizens all across the empire not to throw away fruit and vegetable seeds, and leftovers that can be sprouted. We will take food scraps; carrots, turnips, potatoes, garlic, tomatoes, and we will sprout them before we plant them. The Immortals will have their own garden, and their own cook who will prepare their meals in the cheapest, tastiest way possible."

Memukkan nodded furiously. "I will right away, Your Highness!"

Megabyzus smiled. "Impressive, Your Highness, but my men also like meat. It gives them strength."

A loud shriek came from the challenged soldier as he brought his sagaris down hard in the center of the lion's head. The lion roared loudly before dropping to the ground in a lifeless heap.

Xerxes knitted his eyebrows. "We use pigs." He turned again to Memukkan. "Order the citizens not to throw away any food leftovers, not even a crumb. We pay the poor two bronze pieces a week to sort it. Pigs eat anything."

Megabyzus smiled. "Perfect." He bowed low as Xerxes turned to leave.

"One more question," said Xerxes as he turned to Megabyzus.

"What is it, Your Highness?" asked Megabyzus.

"What will you do with the dead lion?" asked Xerxes, pointing to the lifeless creature.

Megabyzus gave a broad smile. "We will eat him!" he laughed.

Memukkan looked mortified.

"As you wish," said Xerxes nodding grimly. His lips were set in a straight firm line. He turned, and with one final sweep of the royal cape, he and Memukkan were gone.

Hadassah

CHAPTER FOUR

Hadassah shivered. The early morning air seeped through the warmth of her outer garments, slowly soaking its way into her pores. The cool breeze was nothing compared to the stone-cold demeanor of the executioner on the platform. Artanos stood bound tightly with thick, impenetrable ropes that clasped his hands and feet firmly together.

"You are, this day, charged with treason in the first degree," read a short, skinny man. "You are hereby sentenced to punishment by the boats." His high-pitched voice trembled as it squeaked out the sentence dealt out to the one being charged.

Hadassah gasped.

Artanos' eyes were tightly closed, and as he fervently muttered to his god, he shook with fear like the many that are shaken by the smell of death. Once a high official, he now lay on the wooden platform, his body shredded and prodded. He wore a single undergarment and, stripped of his riches, he clutched a tiny gold statue.

Hadassah looked around. The crowd was thick, so thick that people pushed and shoved one another to get a glimpse of the execution. Everyone in Susa was present by order of the king. She squeezed Mordecai's hand as she watched a small boat be brought onto the platform.

From where she stood with Mordecai, Hadassah spotted As-Ho. He glared at her. Her face burned with embarrassment, however deep down, she rejoiced. Mordecai had denied his marriage request, and shortly afterward he had left in a huff. Slowly she tore her gaze away from As-Ho's stony stare.

"You sought to lay hands on our king!" a short, stout man roared, violently shaking his fist at the platform. A tomato flew through the air and hit Artanos, smacking him squarely in the face. He did not move. Two muscular men lifted Artanos high above the platform before tying him to the boat. His hands were tied to the helm and his feet to the rear.

"How dare you threaten our king!" an angry, dark-haired woman yelled. Two more tomatoes hit Artanos in the head this time. Then Artanos' mouth was forced open. He struggled and shook his head violently as milk and honey were forced into his gut, mercilessly stuffing him.

"Long live the king!" the short, stout man shouted. He pumped his fist towards the crowd, and everyone joined in his chant. "Long live the king! Long live the king!" Several more tomatoes flew through the air. The same two men then spread the sticky honey over Artanos' bloody body, particularly on his eyes and stomach.

Hadassah shuddered. She was familiar with this particular punishment. After being forced to drink more milk and honey, Artanos would be left to rot on the open ocean in the hot burning sun for days. The milk and honey would then give him diarrhea. This would attract insects of all sorts. Flies and maggots would be the first to feast until the horrid smell of his body would travel to vultures and other predators who too would feast upon him even before death took him.

Suddenly, a hush fell over the crowd. Hadassah strained to see what all the fuss was about. A stream of purple and a flash of diamonds and rubies were all she could see. It was the king! She tip-toed but could not make out anything else for the crowd was too thick.

"This is what happens to those who seek to lay hands on the king!" the firm voice of King Xerxes said. "From now on no one is to approach a Persian king without first being summoned," he continued.

"He or she will be killed immediately. This goes for any man, woman, child or animal."

Mordecai squeezed Hadassah's hand tighter.

"UNLESS," the king shouted, and stopped as his eyes swept the crowd, "Unless the scepter of the king is extended to him, her or it. Then and only then will he, she, or it will be allowed to live!" he finished.

"Long live the king," the crowd shouted.

CHAPTER FIVE

"How dare you defy me when summoned?" Xerxes shouted, bursting through the doors of the bedchamber. He stomped back and forth, clearly enraged, while Vashti looked on in dismay. He was still intoxicated. The Moon Feast, which was held for his officials and administrators, had lasted three days. It was a grand celebration that commemorated the latest feat of the armies of Persia and Media. They had conquered one more province, a welcome addition to his empire. His empire now consisted of one hundred and twenty-seven provinces to be exact. It was a time of celebration! Three days of partying meant three days of sublime food, wine, and women.

Xerxes staggered a bit as he zig-zagged his way towards Vashti. No one had dared defy him until now. No one dared to defy the Emperor. He was Shah, Xerxes the Great, Shahanshah and Khshayarsa. His wine goblet smashed into the vanity glass, staining the expensive wood with its rich red contents.

Vashti screamed. "Please, Xerxes! Be reasonable!" She ducked as Xerxes flew into another rage.

"Your job as queen was simple," he said through gritted teeth. He grabbed her arm firmly. "I call, you come!" He was a fairly large man who loomed over her, firm and sure. He commanded attention! Years of military training contributed to his muscular build. The scar near his right eye added to the effect. One was drawn in immediately at the first sight of him. No other in the empire was as striking as he was. He glared down at her, the heat of anger burning through his eyes.

"What do you mean, 'was'?" Her voice quavered for the first time since Xerxes had barged into the room. "Are you threatening my crown?" she said coolly. Vashti straightened up with forced confidence.

This angered Xerxes even more. "Did I ask you to speak?" he said in a low dangerous voice. His grip tightened as he shot her another venomous glare.

"This is the problem with you women these days," he grumbled. "You're too *free,* and when given an inch, you take a mile!"

She looked away in disgust. Her eyes were lined with black ink, and her false lashes protruded from her face, stiff with firming liquid-clay. She was dripping in royal jewels, and her false nails extended at least four inches. Her face was a sea of black drained goo. It was evident she had been crying.

Xerxes had never really seen her with such minimal confidence. Queen-ship had made her obnoxious over the years, and her latest stunt was a real blow to Xerxes' ego. These days she usually spent her time giving feasts of her own, surrounded by food, wine and the high-pitched giggles of her handmaidens.

"Your order was to come naked!" Vashti winced, clearly in pain.

"You are lying, you deceitful woman!" Xerxes shouted. "Don't you dare play victim with me," he said in a daring voice. The past three days had been a blur. He sat down slowly and held his head in his hands as he tried to remember the past couple of hours.

He had been feasting his eyes upon the unclothed dancer, when Haman, one of his administrators had approached. Haman was a tall, slim fellow with long, bony fingers. He was slinky and snake-like, and many described him as slippery and conniving. Popular for his manipulation and lies, people wondered how he made it into such high office. He was hungry for power, and the word on the street was that he was running again. "Beautiful, isn't she?" he yelled in a way that demanded an audience.

Xerxes had chuckled loudly.

"She's nothing compared to my wife," Haman shouted above the loud music. He grinned at Xerxes.

"No woman in the entire empire compares to mine," Xerxes proposed boldly. He gave an intoxicating laugh.

Haman's demeanor became serious. "Prove it," he said. He poked Teresh, one of the king's eunuchs, who sat beside the king.

As if on cue, Teresh got up and clapped his hands loudly. "Prove it, prove it!" he said in a singsong voice. "Prove it, prove it!" the entire table of drunk generals and council members started singing. Slowly but surely, the entire party joined in.

"Give the order. Tell Queen Vashti her presence is requested at the Moon Feast. She must prove what I have said," Xerxes shouted to Haman, who then hurried off to give the instructions to the eunuchs.

Moments later, one of the eunuchs returned with news of Vashti's refusal.

"Clearly no woman in the empire compares to the Queen," Haman smirked. "For no woman dare insult her husband the way the queen insults you, Your Majesty." His lips curled into a snarl.

Silence consumed the festivities right before an enraged and clearly embarrassed Xerxes flew into a rage. The fun ended. The party came to an abrupt end, and the guests were dismissed.

Xerxes, now in Vashti's bedchamber, realized his mistake. He held his head in his hands. His locks fell down around his broad shoulders which now slumped in defeat. This was a nightmare! He never meant for his wife to be paraded undressed before his men. However, the insult had already been made. Vashti had already imprinted a stamp of offense on his reputation in front of the entire kingdom.

"You could have shown up dressed. It would not have made a difference. But to not show up at all exceeds marital breaches far beyond what one could imagine," he said furiously.

"I did what I knew was right," Vashti proposed boldly. "You and your drunken generals had no right to demand I be paraded in front of the entire kingdom just to satisfy your perverted appetites."

"*Your* job was to lead by example alongside myself the king as I rule the kingdom of Persia and the one hundred and twenty-seven provinces," he said informatively as if this was foreign information.

"From India to Ethiopia, I have ruled the Northern Kingdoms, Southern Islands, Eastern Realms and Western Monarchies with an iron fist. How will they view me now? I can't even keep my own *wife* under control." He shook uncontrollably as he tried not to explode all over again. "Do you know what you have done, woman?" he growled. "I'll be the laughing stock of the kingdom!" He shook his head grimly. "To be viewed as weak could even threaten this empire."

Haman had a point. A wife's disobedience was an insult to her husband. This being said, Xerxes was "king." If one believed he could defy a man of such power and magnitude, one could believe that he could get away with anything! It was unheard of. Xerxes knew gossip was already beginning to spread as the palace staff whispered about the recent events that had unfolded. He had to fix this and meeting with the high council was the only way to come up with the right solution.

He threw Vashti one last toxic glare and left the bedchamber in a huff.

As he left, he silently vowed never to drink to the point where his judgment would be clouded ever again. A mistake well spent on his behalf was a lesson well learned. This error of his may very well cost him his empire. He would do whatever it took to fix this.

CHAPTER SIX

The local exotic meat merchant eyed Hadassah as she passed by the stalls of the bazaar. "Crabs, rabbit legs, pig ears, bear brains!" shouted the plump, heavily bearded man. "Get your delicious snake eyeballs here!" he shouted again, louder this time.

Hadassah pulled her chador tighter around her, careful not to let any of her hair fall out, and hurried past him. The salty spray of the sea was refreshing on her face, and the smell of livestock mixed with fish and spices and fresh dung engulfed her at once.

"I have the tastiest bull testicles at half price, miss," he shouted after her. "They're great in soup!"

"No, thank you," she said firmly. She subtly checked to make sure her coin pouch was still intact before tightening her grip on the basket she carried. One had to be careful when at the market, besides swindling pick-pocketing was also common at the bazaar.

"Sugar, sea salt, and spices miss?" A young girl smiled sweetly at Hadassah.

"Hadassah smiled back.

"My mommy has sugar, sea salt, and spices," she informed Hadassah pointing to a tall woman at the far end of the stall. "Mommy, the pretty lady wants to buy something!"

"Ok, Yasmin," the woman laughed as she came over to Hadassah.

"Do you barter?" asked Hadassah entering the stall.

"That depends on what you have to trade." The woman smiled at her.

"Uh, I have one skin of fresh goat's milk, half a pound of cheese, quarter pound of butter and some wild berries from my garden," replied Hadassah.

"That will do," said the woman. "I'll give you one pound of sugar, one pound of sea salt and half a pound of a spice of your choice," she said as she started to package the sugar.

"Ok fine. I'll take half a pound of Egyptian curry powder please," said Hadassah.

"Very well," she replied. She measured, weighed and then rolled Hadassah's requests into tiny tight packages.

Another customer entered, and Hadassah thanked the woman then left with her sugar and spices tightly bundled into the basket she carried. The noise of the bazaar thronged around her again as she stepped out of the stall.

"Fresh fish!" yelled a short, bony man.

"How much does your fish cost?" asked Hadassah.

"One bronze piece per pound," he sneered.

"Are they fresh?" she asked.

"The freshest in the market today, Miss," he replied. He grinned, exposing a row of missing front teeth.

"When were they caught?" asked Hadassah, giving them a closer look.

He squinted at her. "They were caught this morning, now are you buying or not lady?" he replied impatiently.

"I would like one pound of herring please," said Hadassah.

"Only one poun..." His sentence trailed as he went off to package Hadassah's fish. He grumbled as he weighed them out to exactness.

A dirty young woman with seven dirty children shuffled into the stall. She began to examine first the salmon and the turbot.

The fish merchant grumbled as he wrapped up Hadassah's herring and then stretched forth his right hand towards Hadassah.

"There," she said. She rolled her eyes as she placed the bronze piece into his outstretched hand.

"I'm not a swindler," she said, taking the package from him and tucking it safely away into her basket.

"HEY! YOU!" yelled the fish merchant. The woman with the seven children jumped at his outburst. Her coal-streaked face now wore a look of horror. "SCRAM!" the merchant yelled, his face red with rage.

"I just want a pound of fish guts," she pleaded.

"That will be half a bronze piece for a pound of fish guts," he sneered. "Better yet that will be one bronze piece today because yer didn't cover yer bill yesterday!"

"Please kind sir," she begged, as she held the half bronze piece towards him.

"Pay yer bills, Miss, this isn't charity!" He snatched the money and pocketed the coin. "Now, scram!"

She began to cry as she shuffled out of the stall.

"Is that how you treat your customers?" Hadassah asked in an angry voice.

"That is how I treat people who don't pay their bill," he scoffed.

"I don't want to purchase anything from you!" Hadassah said angrily.

"Sorry Miss, no refund," he mocked.

"I would like a bushel of salmon and a bushel of cod please," said a smooth, watery voice.

Hadassah turned suddenly. A tall, thin, bony man with long bony fingers and a false grin was standing directly behind her.

"Pardon me, pretty lady," he said in a sly voice.

"Haman!" exclaimed the fish merchant bowing low before pulling out his best salmon steaks and cods. "I have been looking forward to your arrival! I only save the best for you!"

Hadassah's pulse quickened. She pulled her chador tighter around her, hugged her basket and quickly made her way out of the stall.

"Put it on my tab," Haman was saying.

"That is most certainly not a problem my lord, not a problem," the fish merchant sang in his friendliest voice.

Hadassah fled the stall as quickly as she could. Something about Haman gave her the creeps. Her pulse slowed, and she hurried on towards a brightly decorated stall filled with fabrics.

"Hadassah!" a middle-aged woman greeted.

"Hello, Mrs. Jaiylo! I have your order," said Hadassah. She entered the stall and hugged Mrs. Jaiylo.

"Oh good," she said. "I'm so glad." She rubbed her hands together in excitement. "Can I see?" she asked.

Hadassah grinned as she carefully pulled a bright blue dress and a bright yellow dress out of her basket.

"Ohhh!" exclaimed Mrs. Jaiylo. "I love it! The nobles will love them too Hadassah! They spend a fortune on your designs!"

Hadassah smiled as Mrs. Jaiylo removed two gold pieces from her pouch and placed them into her hand.

"I also have something for you." She turned and began to rummage through a nearby pile of fabric. "I thought of you the moment I received this in my shipment," she said, retrieving a red silk fabric with pretty gold detailing.

"I love it!" said Hadassah.

"Here you go, dear. I'll give it to you for two bronze pieces. You can pay me the next time you come," she said, giving Hadassah's shoulder a light squeeze.

"Thank you, Mrs. Jaiylo."

She folded the fabric and carefully placed it in her basket away from the fish she had bought.

"I also want to give you these," said Mrs. Jaiylo. She held out three tiny golden buttons. "I want you to have them Hadassah."

"Wow, they are beautiful! I couldn't..." Her voice trailed.

"Nonsense," said Mrs. Jaiylo. "They're from Jerusalem," she said her voice barely above a whisper. "My father gave them to me before he returned to help rebuild the wall."

"Why didn't you go?" asked Hadassah.

"I have a life here, and I don't remember Jerusalem. I left there a slave, and now I have a solid life here with a prominent business. Under King Cyrus' reign, God blessed us just as he had promised to."

Hadassah nodded. "I must get back now. Thank you so much for the buttons." She secured the three gold buttons inside her money pouch.

"See you next time, Hadassah." She waved as Hadassah left the stall.

Hadassah noticed that the bazaar was less busy than before when she stepped out of the stall. She made her way towards home, slowing when she recognized the woman with the seven children. She was still pleading with the fish merchant, who was now purple in the face with frustration and rage. Hadassah cautiously removed one of her gold coins from her pouch before securing it again.

"Hey!" she called as she walked up to them. "I want you to take this gold coin under one condition," she said to the woman. "Do not purchase anything from him!" She shoved the coin into her hand and glared at the fish merchant before walking away, leaving them both stunned and speechless.

King Xerxes

CHAPTER SEVEN

Xerxes tried to reel in his anger as the heavy brass doors of the throne room opened. His upper lip trembled the way it did when he was mad beyond words. He leaned against the gold throne that his forefathers had fought so hard to obtain. He closed his eyes as the dynamics of his family's dynasty flashed through his head. Every detail explained to him over and over again from the moment he was old enough to understand until the sweat, blood, and tears became a part of his very being. This had ensured he never forgot the importance of his family's goal of world dominance. They must always be number one. They must be the head and never the tail. *One-hundred and twenty-seven provinces and counting*, he thought to himself.

"Your Highness, we present to you Queen Vashti," a guard announced before reclaiming his place near the huge brass doors.

Vashti glided through the doors with a coolness that grated Xerxes' nerves.

"Does she even realize what she has done?" he thought to himself.

Her yellow dress painfully reminded Xerxes of the many enjoyable times that they had together in the past.

"You summoned me, Your Highness?" She bowed low. Her pale hair fell around her shoulders the way Xerxes always admired.

"Your actions have forced my hand," Xerxes began.

"How do you mean, Your Highness?" she asked calmly as if she knew what was coming next.

"Your defiance cannot go unpunished!" he said, his voice getting louder with each word.

There was silence as the soldiers shut the brass doors.

"Have you nothing to say in your defense?"

"Would it make a difference, Xerxes?" she asked. "It seems to me your mind is already made up."

Xerxes closed his eyes. He had to dig deep to find patience and civility. Everything inside him was holding him back from clobbering Vashti.

"The Achaemenid Empire was a dynasty foreseen by my grandfather King Cyrus the Great. It was a goal that he achieved through hard work. It is an achievement meant to be preserved and upheld not thrown away because a lover's quarrel compromised it," he said, looking angrier with each word. "Do you understand this?" he asked.

"Yes," said Vashti quietly.

"Every war was fought with one thing in mind." He looked her over in disgust. "Our LEGACY."

"Xerxes, I come before you as your wife," Vashti sniffled. Her first humble action since entering the throne room. "Please forgive me and have mercy. It will never happen again. I promise."

"Do you understand the position you have placed me in Vashti?" he shouted rising from his throne. "I cannot show mercy! I will be perceived as WEAK!" He circled his throne and held his head. "And then you walk in here calm and composed and with every coolness in the kingdom. Do you even care?"

"I care, Xerxes, I do!" Vashti sobbed. "I am a queen Xerxes. I am trained not to show my feelings when things are falling apart on the inside."

"You stand before me composed after placing my kingdom at risk?"

"Please be reasonable, Xerxes," she pleaded.

"I *have* been reasonable!" he spat. "You should have been beheaded at the banquet with every guest as a witness!"

"You're cruel. You've become cruel!" She sniffled again before becoming somewhat composed. "Power has really done a number on you!"

"You still don't understand what is at stake, do you?" he asked in a dangerous, low voice. "Until I decide your fate, you will take up residence in the dungeons with nothing but darkness to keep you company. I suggest you burn every bridge that lies between us because I never want to see you again."

"Xerxes, I still love you!" Vashti pleaded.

Xerxes shut his ears, and his heart to her cries as he dished out the coldness that was expected of him.

"Guards, get her out of my sight!"

CHAPTER EIGHT

Hadassah's hair swayed in the breeze as she ran with great speed away from the small cottage she shared with her cousin Mordecai. The fabric of her simple dress danced in the wind.

Mordecai chased after her to the best of his ability.

Mordecai and Hadassah lived in a humble cottage behind a thicket near the river in Susa in a place called, "Hunting Valley." Most Jews lived in Hunting Valley. Beyond Hunting Valley was Frostbite Mountain—a dark, disturbing place rumored to be filled with strange, dark and deadly creatures.

Mordecai was a hard worker and gave one hundred percent to his job. At the end of each week, he would put aside one silver coin in order to purchase a better place to live that was closer to the city.

"Wait up!" Mordecai shouted, breathlessly trying to keep up.

He had gained quite a bit of weight over the past year, due to Hadassah's fantastic cooking. Every week there was a new cuisine to try. To make things worse, he was born with his right leg shorter than his left, so he was considered a misfit. He was not a pleasant sight to many. However, he bore a good heart in his chest, and that was all that mattered.

Hadassah hurried ahead. Mordecai had woken up early and scurried after her at the crack of dawn.

His newest parenting technique involved the rule that she had to account for every second of her day. Hadassah had been unable to give an account of the first hour she disappeared. Mordecai swore that he would find out exactly what she had been up to. His determination and drive had brought them to this moment of cat and mouse. He had caught her sneaking fish into the basket she now cradled in her arms. Hadassah had jumped in astonishment when he caught her. The look on her face caused him to feel so guilty about startling her. However, he was determined to quell his suspicions.

"What is she going to do with that fish?" he thought to himself. "Fish was eaten at the end of the week as a treat. Today is Thursday!"

"Please stop following me!" Hadassah begged. She thought Mordecai's obsession with her safety was becoming downright ridiculous. "I can take care of myself," she assured him, her eyes widely pleading with him. "You're going to cause breakfast to be late," she added.

"Fine!" Mordecai agreed quickly. The taste of yesterday's dinner still lingered on his lips. There had been curried goat topped with the spices she had grown herself in her garden. This was accompanied by her famous cornmeal, with a side of lentils, beans, pomegranates and corn rolled in light, sweet dough. Sweet, fresh goat's milk had washed their meal down. Dessert had been figs rolled in dough and generously topped with fresh goat's milk and honey. Hadassah certainly had a gift. She could take ingredients from meager to great.

Hadassah usually took meals from scanty to grand. Mordecai was often taken aback by her ability to think outside of the box. Recently despite her young age, she had suggested that she should help him pay taxes. Mordecai had simply nodded and waved her away with a smile. The next day he got a stunning revelation when she brought him her first gold coin as her contribution.

"How d-d-did you…?" Mordecai had managed to stammer out.

"I sold the fig tarts I made this morning, along with the dresses I had been working on to Mrs. Jaiylo," she responded as if it was nothing at all.

Mordecai's eyes widened in amazement. The Jaiylos were upstanding citizens in an upscale neighborhood. He was impressed that she had targeted the upper-class community.

"I made two," she added.

"Two dresses?" Mordecai asked.

"Two gold coins," she corrected.

"Where is the other?" Mordecai asked trying his hardest not to sound too controlling.

"There was a lady at the market who could not cover her bill. She had seven small children. She needed it more than we did," she had said calmly.

Mordecai smiled to himself. She was a good woman. He admired her kindness and strength. He felt a weight lift off him as he remembered these moments that were so pure and genuine and filled with such goodness. He felt guilty about suspecting she was up to something cheeky. Slowly he let go of his worries as he made his way back to the house.

At a young age, Hadassah had mastered the art of supply and demand. Word soon got out about her talents. The women raved about her food and clothes. They sent orders every week for Hadassah to fill. This kept her busy; however, despite this, she never seemed satisfied.

Mordecai loved her with all of his heart and taught her every day everything he knew about the Lord. She was almost at the age to start attending the selection balls in order to choose a proper suitor for courting. Hadassah did not seem very interested, and although this sat more than well with Mordecai, he knew that the time would eventually come when she would have to begin courting.

As he made his way back to the house, his mind wandered to the conversation they had over last night's dinner. "Will you be attending any of the selected balls this year?" Mordecai asked.

Hadassah scrunched her face and laughed. "I'm happy, but I'm not ready to be that happy," she said. "Do you know what I mean?"

"No!" Mordecai responded in genuine confusion.

"I'm still working on me and who I am as a person. I must be able to hold myself to the same standard I hold him to," she replied.

"What is it you want from your mate?" he asked. "What are you looking for?"

"I need him to genuinely be my friend, someone I can share my deepest secrets with. I need someone willing to protect me with his life. I need a teammate, someone with whom I can share projects, purchase property, as well as share responsibilities and achievements. I want someone who thinks big, who has character, pride, and integrity—someone who exercises decency and possesses morals and wisdom; someone who can guide me financially, and who is emotionally available and stable; someone who will be at my side at balls, awards and recognition ceremonies. I want someone who has achieved on his own and does not feel threatened by the status I seek to achieve in the universe; he needs to be someone who will not be intimidated by my global footprint, or the legacy I aspire to leave behind. He must be a lover who will satisfy me from beginning to end. He must realize that God is the source of his life and daily gives back to his Creator; he has to be someone who knows how to handle himself in the worlds of both nobility and poverty. I need a whole person. I want a man who strives for excellence in every aspect of his life—

a man who will give me a relationship far above mediocrity, that is, a relationship that exceeds all expectations. I want a relationship where we both excel together. I want a marriage of excellence."

Mordecai stared at her, too stunned to utter a word.

"I need this not only for the stability of my future family but also for the sake of my sanity. I need a marriage that not only grows but blossoms," she finished.

Mordecai had never felt prouder. He grabbed her shoulders, looked her square in the eyes and said, "Then Hadassah go after your dreams like a war general going after the enemy; research, scheme, and strategize to do whatever it takes to make that dream a reality!"

Mordecai always made reference to the war and the army. He had always dreamed of being in the army but dreaming about it was all that he could do. The condition of his body would never see him fit enough to even be considered to fight for the empire. "Some of us cannot even dare to dream," he said sadly.

EEEEkkkk! A strange noise pierced the air, interrupting Mordecai's thoughts.

EEEkkk! The clear shrill sound rang out again. Mordecai froze. "Was it a wild animal?" This part of Susa was fairly safe. However, one could never be too careful. He tried to make out exactly where the sound was coming from.

Mordecai followed the noise closely. It was coming from an area near the ravine behind the waterfall. Balancing himself on the slippery rocks, he leaned in, making out a soft whisper.

"Shhh," the voice whispered softly.

Just then the rock gave way, causing him to fall into the ravine.

Mordecai looked up in dismay. Sweating bullets, his heart plummeted. He began to shake with fear. There stood Hadassah, and there towering over her was a DRAGLE.

CHAPTER NINE

"**I**, KING Xerxes gave Vashti a command and she refused to OBEY it! What does the law say regarding how we should punish her?" Xerxes' voice boomed throughout the courtroom. He had awakened all seven of his officials in the middle of the night to deal with the matter at hand. The rain beat down hard upon the palace. It was a dark, stormy night. Lightning danced across the skies while thunder rolled heavily in the background, creating an atmosphere even more theatrical than the scene that was beginning to unfold deep within the court chambers of the palace.

All seven officials stood trembling before the king, too afraid to speak. Shethar began to stammer something no one could understand.

Xerxes shook his head. "Speak up! Time is passing, and we cannot allow this to spiral out of control!"

Memukkan was the first to gain control of his tongue. "Your Majesty...errr, Shethar here was just wondering if you were still..." his voice trailed off.

Xerxes leaned in. "What?" His rage was now slightly cooled. He did not mean to take his anger out on these men. They had helped him through many hard times when it came to matters related to law and order. Their support and strategy had aided him in winning many battles as well as ensuring that the citizens of his empire receive the justice they deserve. Reigning was not easy, and he owed these men for their years of committed service to him and his empire.

"Ugghh, you cannot be intoxicated at a court hearing Your Majesty," Memukkan finished quickly. Shethar nodded in agreement.

Xerxes smiled. Despite his slightly twisted tooth, charm seeped through his grin. "Shethar, I can assure you that the only thing I am intoxicated with is the desire to fix the situation at hand."

All seven eunuchs sighed in relief. Xerxes beamed. These men truly cared about him. He was in good hands.

The next few hours were spent poring over the royal scrolls. Scroll after scroll was opened and still, nothing gave reference to what the consequences would be when a queen disobeys the king's command.

"Has anyone found anything yet?" Xerxes asked. "This is tiring! We are wasting valuable time!"

"Not yet, your Majesty," Admatha said hesitantly. He was the quiet one of the bunch. He was so quiet and humble that this forced Xerxes to chain his growing anger. As his anger grew, his patience was wearing thinner and thinner.

"I will be back in one hour," Xerxes said impatiently. "When I return, I expect a solution to this despicable mess," he said in disgust.

"B-b-but Your Majesty. This could take days..." Tarshish gasped.

Meres, Carshena, and Marsena looked on, wide-eyed.

"Find something!" Xerxes commanded firmly. "Find anything!" And with one sweep of his royal cloak, he was gone.

The seven eunuchs exchanged looks. They were elders, and there were times when the king's free spirit left them awestruck. They each turned back to their scrolls when Memukkan gasped.

"This is it!" He opened the scroll wider and pressed it against the table. "This is Vashti's coronation oath."

Shethar looked blankly at him. "How will that tell us which punishment will fit the crime?"

Memukkan read aloud. "I, Vashti Annelle of Susa, do solemnly swear to rule alongside my husband, never above him and to uphold the standards of the empire to the highest esteem. Most importantly, I vow to lead by a perfect example for every province, creed, and race. This my pledge shall be, until the end of my reign."

Shethar scratched his head in confusion.

"She broke her vows to her husband and the empire. She has insulted the king and his empire. She has not been a perfect example of a good role model as the Queen of Persia. She has threatened the empire. Women from every province, creed, and race will disobey their husbands because of Vashti's actions." He gave a dramatic pause and looked around nervously as if someone might be listening. "Queen Vashti must be impeached," he whispered.

The king entered at that moment. "Your Majesty, we have something," Memukkan informed him.

King Xerxes smiled. "Very good," he said. "I can't wait to hear what you all have come up with to fix this problem."

CHAPTER TEN

Mordecai sputtered with rage as he stamped from the ravine back to the small cottage he shared with Hadassah. "HOW COULD YOU KEEP SUCH A SECRET FROM ME?" Mordecai shouted. He wasn't sure what was going on at first, but Hadassah's extended hand and the fish that hung from it was all the explanation he needed. He was more hurt than angry. However, when he regained his footing, he stormed from the ravine back to the cottage, going as fast as his dumpy legs could carry him.

What was a dragle doing in Susa? He thought to himself. They were supposed to be extinct! The half-dragon, half-eagle bred monsters had been banned by King Cyrus many decades ago after two villages had mysteriously burned to the ground. This one seemed to be a pure-bred, about fifteen feet tall with wings that extended far beyond measure. She was white as snow with blue piercing eyes.

"Mordecai, I am so sorry!" Hadassah whispered.

"Are you?" Mordecai replied, trying to keep his voice level down. "I gave you a million chances to tell me what you were up to!" He paced back and forth, clearly distraught. "How long has this been going on?"

"I've had her from she was a baby," Hadassah said on the verge of tears. She loved Mordecai and had not intentionally hurt him.

"A b-b-baby," Mordecai stammered in disbelief.

"I found her behind the ravine. She had a thorn in her foot. I nursed her back to health." She blinked back tears.

"You did what?" Mordecai replied mortified. He was afraid to ask anything else. Dragles were a forbidden species. Xerxes' grandfather had waged war on them, driving them into extinction. To learn that Hadassah had *nursed* one back to health meant she had signed her death warrant.

"Her name is Hydra, and if you would just get to know her, you would see that she is really a sweetheart," Hadassah pleaded.

Mordecai limped frantically around the kitchen looking for the herb they used to put the chickens to sleep before slaughtering them. He had little knowledge of how it worked, but hopefully, if he used enough, it would work on the dragle also.

BRAM, BRAM, BRAM, BRAM! "OPEN UP IN THE NAME OF THE KING!"

Both Mordecai and Hadassah looked up startled. Had they been found out? Mordecai limped to the door, afraid to face what was on the other side. He motioned to Hadassah not to say anything. She nodded in agreement.

"King Xerxes of the greatest dynasty has a decree. Let all under the sound of my voice heed this decree," one of the two soldiers, who stood outside, bellowed.

Mordecai forced himself not to roll his eyes as the taller of the two bowed low before Hadassah. There was no doubt that Hadassah was beautiful. Her hair flowed down her back in long, black, thick waves. Her cheeks and lips were rosy. Her skin was flawless. She was slender, yet curvy in all the right places, and she bore a subtle innocence that attracted many to her.

"What is this about?" Mordecai asked. Chills ran up and down his spine.

"I King Xerxes, Emperor of Persia, inform you that Queen Vashti shall be savagely punished for her rebellious actions against The King. I declare that women of every creed and race will submit to their husbands. Those who follow in Vashti's footsteps will suffer an unimaginable fate as she will."

EEEkkk!

Mordecai swallowed deeply.

"What was that?" one of the soldiers asked.

Mordecai let out something that sounded more like a whimper than a response. He wanted to hold his head in his hands.

"Oh, dear!" he stammered. He could feel Hadassah beside him trembling. He hoped she would not give them away.

EEEkkk!

"Probably a wild bird…" said Mordecai, his voice trailing off.

"That's no wild bird," said the soldier who had winked at Hadassah. He grinned at Hadassah, seizing this as the perfect opportunity to try and win her over through a heroic act.

With unsheathed swords, the soldiers carefully made their way around the side of the cottage. They were not sure what they were up against.

Two seconds later, they came sprinting back towards Mordecai and Hadassah, red-faced and sweating buckets. The fear in their eyes told Mordecai that their secret had been found out.

EEEkkk!

The soldier who had winked at Hadassah was gasping for breath and shouting for backup.

Everything seemed to happen in slow motion after that. Armed with chains, six more soldiers joined the first two in the quest to capture the perceived danger.

Mordecai's heart pounded. He hoped that they would not be arrested because the dragle was found on their property.

Hadassah stood trembling, unable to say a word! She was so shaken up that Mordecai had to wrap her up in his arms. He knew that if she spilled her tears, she would give them both away.

Thankfully, the soldiers viewed his loving act as a sign of protection rather than comfort.

"My lady, you are now safe," the tall soldier said, and then bowed again before they led the dragle off in chains. So, just like that they were gone, leaving Hadassah in despair and Mordecai thankful beyond measure that they weren't thrown into the dungeons.

CHAPTER ELEVEN

Xerxes leaned forward in his stirrup and pressed his body against his horse. "Just a little further, Lightning," he urged the stallion. Her sleek, black, shiny coat gleamed. Her nostrils flared. "There she is," he whispered to her softly. He had spotted a young deer earlier by the stream of life and had chased her into the thickest part of the forest. Deer meat was always appreciated back at the palace. Xerxes expertly slowed the horse down before bringing her to a complete stop. Lightning pawed the ground and thrust her head back. Hunting excited her just as much as it did him. "Easy girl," he said softly. He raised his bow and arrow. He watched as the deer moved with such agility and grace. He skillfully placed the arrow in the bow and pulled it back as far as he could before he released.

"Right between the eyes," he said to himself as he watched the deer collapse in a heap.

He sat in silence and allowed the stillness of the forest to soothe his grated nerves. The empty feeling inside of his chest seemed even hollower than before. The pit of his stomach felt heavy with sorrow. He missed Vashti terribly. Even his body grieved her absence.

Xerxes turned suddenly as the sound of horses' hooves resounded throughout the forest.

"Your Majesty!" Megabyzus exclaimed. "This way!" he shouted to the approaching men from behind.

"Isn't this a little dramatic?" asked Xerxes. Hundreds of Persian Immortals surrounded him at the command of Megabyzus.

"Your Majesty," called Memukkan carefully maneuvering his horse through the only path the Immortals had left open.

Right behind him were Carshena, Shethar, Admatha, Tarshish, Meres, and Marsena.

"I hope you brought wine," called Xerxes. He looked on as the Council of Seven surrounded him.

"Your majesty, we were so concerned about your safety that wine was not on our minds," said Marsena. "Do forgive us."

"You should not run off into the woods to hunt alone Your Majesty," said Tarshish.

"Killing things makes me feel better," Xerxes said in a low voice. "I need counseling," He guided Lightning through the soldiers towards a secluded area near the stream. The Council of Seven followed him.

"What troubles you, oh, King?" asked Admatha.

"Is it Vashti?" Meres asked.

"You were most gracious when you banished her," said Carshena. "A wife like that deserves to be hanged. Disobedience should never go without a memorable punishment."

Admatha nodded in agreement as he tried to calm his horse. "If she had been my wife, I would have had her beheaded," he said. "Better yet, you should have cut her tongue out of her head and let her wear it on a string around her neck. She would have never said the word no again ever."

"If she was my wife, I would have had her split in two," growled Shethar.

"No, no, no." Tarshish held up his hand in disagreement. "Condemning her to the walk of shame throughout the streets of Persia would have sufficed." He chuckled. "That would have taught her a great lesson – not to mention we would still have had a queen."

"Children are taught lessons, not grown adults," argued Marsena. "Vashti should have known better. He should have tied her up and made her fulfill her duty as queen." He laughed. "That would have been the greatest lesson of all. When you are summoned, you come with no rebuttal."

"Can you imagine a *woman* disobeying a command?" asked Meres who was still in disbelief of what had taken place in the banquet hall. "I would have broken every bone in her body," he roared.

They all began to argue loudly.

"Silence," said Xerxes. "Walk with me, Memukkan," he ordered as he guided his horse further along the river to a hill that overlooked the city, away from the others who had silently begun to argue among themselves once again.

Memukkan carefully guided his horse behind Xerxes', then alongside him.

Xerxes looked out towards the city deep in thought. "Have you ever been in love?" he finally asked. "How do you get past the pain of loss?"

"Time heals all wounds," Memukkan responded. "We have always taught you that with growth comes great discomfort."

"It is almost unbearable," Xerxes replied.

"Can I share a story with you, Your Highness?"

"By all means," Xerxes replied.

"There was once a woman whom I loved dearly, beyond measure, if I may add," began Memukkan. He paused and took a breath before starting again. "We had met at one of the Selection Balls. She had caught my eye from a great distance. I still remember the bright yellow dress she wore." He paused again and smiled subtly. "Her smile was even brighter!" he said. "I will never forget how we snuck out to get away from everyone. It was her idea, of course. She was adventurous. She was quite the opposite of me." He laughed loudly. "We talked about everything that night. We connected so well. It felt so real and meant to be."

Xerxes leaned in, hanging onto Memukkan's every word and anxious to know where the story was going to take him.

"After the selection ball, I told my father that I had found the woman I wanted to marry." He paused and smiled. "I did not have any solid information about her. As the conversation between my father and I unfolded, it turned out, I didn't know anything beyond her name and the adventurous dreams she had." He paused again. "I spent months looking for her. I sought her out with every effort I had within me."

"Did you find her?" asked Xerxes.

"Yes."

"Well, good for you," replied Xerxes.

"As it turned out, she was a frequent wage earner at one of the brothels. She was "The Dark Stallion's" hardest worker. She had died a few weeks earlier. A bacterial infection had claimed her. She had caught it from one of her many customers. Had I been stupid enough to marry her, I would not be here today counseling you."

Xerxes looked on in disbelief.

"Yes, I nearly married a prostitute. Am I proud of that? No. But it was a lesson well learned," said Memukkan.

"It certainly was," replied Xerxes.

"You see, Xerxes; many things will happen to us in this life, and although we may not understand why what we can definitely be certain of is that a greater reason is behind it all. For as our destiny unfolds, a bigger picture comes into focus and it is then, and only then, we shall see that our steps have been purposely pre-calculated all along."

"I just wish I didn't feel so *empty*," Xerxes confessed. "How did you get past your pain?" he asked.

"I decided to purposefully calculate my life, my goals, and dreams. I redirected my focus towards that and that alone. I concentrated on building my legacy. Now I am an advisor to a great king and have been an advisor to many great kings in the past." He patted Xerxes on the back. "A disobedient queen is an unfit queen. Vashti can be replaced. You are the emperor of a kingdom, vast and of magnitude beyond measure! Recognize your power and use it. Do not let grief overwhelm you! Have a selection ball of your own. You shall be able to pick, choose and refuse. After all, you are the King!"

Xerxes nodded in agreement.

"There is far better on your horizon, Your Highness." Memukkan looked over the young king. "You just can't see it yet. You just need to keep moving forward no matter what. One foot in front of the other will get you to your goal. Keep moving. The closer you move towards the horizon, the more you shall see."

Xerxes nodded. "Thank you for sharing your story with me, Memukkan."

"We should get back." He guided his horse over towards the other members of the council. "The others are growing impatient."

"Right behind you, Sire."

"You look better already, Your Majesty," called Shethar. "You must have given our king a good deal of inspiration," he said, directing his focus to Memukkan.

"I can only try, Shethar," said Memukkan.

"So, what's the verdict?" asked Meres. "Are we going to let Megabyzus hunt Vashti down and give her what she rightfully deserves?"

Memukkan shook his head.

Xerxes cleared his throat loudly. "On this day, Vashti is officially behind us. She shall remain banished. On this day and every day after that, we shall move forward, and we shall continue to move forward until the end of time." Xerxes raised his chest slightly. "A disobedient queen is an unfit queen. Therefore, we shall simply find a new queen. We shall choose a queen far more beautiful than Vashti. Issue a royal decree for all young virgins to be brought to the palace. They are to be placed under the charge of Hegai, who will issue beauty treatments until the day I view each young maiden. From this pageant, I shall choose a new queen."

CHAPTER TWELVE

Hadassah's shoulders shook as she sobbed violently into the bedchamber's cotton sheets and pillows. The cot where she lay was soaked with the tears she had fervently cried for hours.

"Chains!" She thought to herself. "How could they treat an animal with such force and vileness?" She shuddered as she remembered the tightness of the chains that bound Hydra firmly in place before being carted away.

"May I come in?" asked a low voice. It was Mordecai.

Hadassah did not feel like being bothered. However, she nodded in agreement.

Mordecai sat on the edge of her cot in silence. "Everything will be okay," he finally said. "You just need to trust God's plan."

"Was it his plan to have her seized and detained in the most violent way possible?" she asked. "That is not very godly." She sniffled. "You have taught me that our God has a gentle nature. Past events have contradicted that beyond measure."

"Her?" asked Mordecai. "You speak about this creature as if she is a person."

"She is a person!" wailed Hadassah.

"I'm not here to talk about the creature," Mordecai said firmly. "I have heard that Vashti is to remain banished. You must prepare to take part in the king's selection process for a new queen."

"I will most certainly not take…." Hadassah began to say.

BRAM, BRAM! "Open up in the name of the king!"

Mordecai signaled to Hadassah to stay put. He hobbled to the door and opened it. A lone soldier began to read a decree.

"I, King Xerxes, issue this royal decree to every province that all young virgins are to be brought to the harem at the palace. From this pageant, I will choose a new queen." He shifted his weight before addressing Mordecai again. "The recent census confirmed that a young lady between the ages of sixteen and thirty resides here. She is to prepare herself to be taken to the palace as a candidate for the king." As quickly as he came, he was gone.

"I do not want to go," came a voice behind Mordecai. Mordecai led Hadassah back to her bedchamber and sat next to her on her cot.

"Hadassah, you have no choice. If the king finds out that you have rebelled against his decree, you will be severely punished. This very pageant is a result of rebellion." He scratched his head thoughtfully. "I have heard the gossip at the palace, and I have thought this over. You must not run from this, Hadassah," he said. "The king will have you beheaded if you run."

"What is the king going to do with an exile?" asked Hadassah. "Not to mention, he may not even like me."

"Where is the confidence you display daily?" replied Mordecai. "If it is meant that he is to like you, then he will like you."

Hadassah shrugged her shoulders with uncertainty.

"Love is full of surprises," said Mordecai looking deep into her eyes. "You will never know what the outcome of a situation will be until you move forward, placing one foot in front of the other."

"I could always go to Jerusalem," Hadassah pointed out.

"The entire kingdom will take part in this pageant. Jerusalem is a part of the kingdom also," responded Mordecai. "You cannot run from this, Hadassah. The king's soldiers will leave no stone unturned when seeking out the best prospect for their king! You are in the census. That includes you!"

"Being a lady is one thing. To be queen is another. Can I handle the pressure of being in the royal family? Back straight, false smile and stiff dresses? I don't think so!"

"If you run from this you will surely be killed!"

Hadassah sat up and sniffled. "I wish I had a choice in the matter."

"What difference does it make?" Mordecai pleaded. "See this as a blessing. Not many girls have the king as a prospect when going through their selection process. The king's soldiers will reach Susa in five to seven days," he said. "We need to prepare you mentally for what you will be up against."

"I'm scared, Mordecai," she confessed.

"Remember fear is temporary but regret is forever," Mordecai replied.

"I've heard that before," she mumbled.

"Now we do not have much time. There are three important things you must remember when you are at the palace."

"I know, I know. Back straight, smile no matter what and always wear the nicest dress," replied Hadassah.

"No!" Mordecai nearly shouted.

"Hadassah laughed. "I'm kidding!"

Mordecai looked lovingly at her. "This is extremely important Hadassah. Please remember what I am about to tell you."

Hadassah nodded solemnly.

"Do not tell anyone that you are a Jew. You will be safer, and no one will judge you based on your background. Trust me. It is better this way."

"Not even the king?" she asked.

"Not even the king."

"But surely honest communication between the king and I should be encouraged," said Hadassah.

"Tell no one that you are a Jew."

"Ok," she replied.

"Secondly, we must change your name,"

"Wait. What? Why?" asked Hadassah.

"The moment you say that your name is Hadassah, they will know that you are Jewish!"

"You're right," she replied thoughtfully. "What shall we change my name to?"

"How about Esther?" said Mordecai. "It means 'star'."

"I don't love it but okay," she replied. "Why do I get the feeling that you have already thought this through?"

"I have prayed and fasted about this," Mordecai confessed.

"I will try and put my best foot forward," said Hadassah.

"Always put your best foot forward no matter what," Mordecai agreed. "Lastly, do not, under any circumstance, seek out that petrifying creature!"

Hadassah's face dropped.

"Do you understand me?" he pressed. "You will be beheaded if caught with that animal."

Hadassah nodded.

"Do we understand each other, Hadassah?" he asked.

"Yes, Mordecai."

"Do we understand each other, Esther?"

She smiled painfully. "Yes, Mordecai."

BRAM, BRAM, BRAM! "Open up in the name of the king!"

CHAPTER THIRTEEN

Sword in hand, Xerxes shifted his weight as he turned towards the enormous metal door. His muscles bulged and tightened as he flung it open with ease. The screams of servants and handmaids could be heard echoing throughout the palace. A chandelier crashed to the floor.

"Your Majesty," Memukkan pleaded breathlessly, "You should be in the safe room!"

Thunder raged outside as a furious Xerxes stormed through the palace. Lightning sparked across the skies identical to the fury Xerxes felt inside.

Xerxes looked down at the short, stubby man as if he had just grown two heads. "Cowards cower!" he nearly shouted at Memukkan.

Memukkan swallowed. He straightened up and pressed his chest out ever so slightly.

Xerxes rolled his eyes. "Go to the safe room, Memukkan," he said with forced composure.

Memukkan stared at him.

"That is an order," he commanded.

Memukkan did not need to be told twice.

Xerxes shook his head as he watched Memukkan scurry off. Never in the history of Xerxes' reign had someone gotten through the palace gates and successfully attacked from the inside. He had taken measure upon measure to ensure that, under no circumstances, this type of attack would take place.

A flash of black sailed pass Xerxes. He squinted hard. He could make out a man with a full scarf around his face that blew out from behind.

Xerxes reached out, grabbing hold of the scarf, and involuntarily yanked the attacker back with immeasurable force. This sent the attacker spiraling backward and dangling in mid-air in Xerxes' arms.

He fought and struggled for about half a minute. He even resorted to biting Xerxes; however, Xerxes, who was determined to regain control of his palace, did not even flinch when the attacker sunk his teeth into his arm.

These men, who were sent to attack the palace from within, were well-trained and quick. They moved much like assassins. Xerxes did not see when the attacker reached up and swiftly untied his scarf, releasing himself from Xerxes' grasp. The attacker ran for half a mile, traveling at the speed of light.

Just then, Haman entered with a group of soldiers. Haman reached up and seized his dagger from his side. Drawing back, he made out the target. "Down you go!" Haman said to himself as he released the weapon. The dagger flew strong and true towards the attacker.

It all happened so fast! Xerxes was more than happy for Haman's gallant act. The attacker lay sputtering on the floor.

Haman was about to throw another dagger when Xerxes stopped him.

"Your Majesty, this man deserves to die," Haman rebutted. However, he did not make any further movements towards him.

Xerxes looked around for the others. They must have fled for all had become still and silent in the palace.

The dagger had sliced through the air into the attacker's lower leg, splitting his bone in two. Blood poured from the wound.

"WHO sent you?" Xerxes shouted, standing heartlessly on top of the wound Haman had just inflicted. It was a good thing Haman did not send the arrow to his heart because Xerxes wanted to interrogate the attacker.

The attacker gave an ear-splitting shriek. "I'll never say!" he cried out, clearly in pain. He bit into the shoulder part of his armor and chewed crazily. He grinned at a stunned Xerxes before his eyes rolled back in his head.

Xerxes shook him ferociously, but there was no response.

He was dead.

"Suicide," said Haman, coming closer to examine the attacker's foaming and blackened mouth. "This man died for his cause," he said dryly.

"Is it safe to come out?" Memukkan asked, peeping out from around the curtain he had been hiding behind.

"Where is our defense?" Xerxes demanded, ignoring Memukkan's question. "Every soldier responsible for defending the castle must meet in the gymnasium, NOW!"

"I-if I m-might say, Your Highness..."

"Spit it out, Memukkan!" Xerxes said angrily.

Memukkan looked more afraid of Xerxes than he was of the attacker.

"No walls have been breached, Your Highness," he finished quickly.

Rage foamed on Xerxes' lips. His eyes burned under the strain of anger. Revenge was forming quickly in his mind. "I want this investigated IMMEDIATELY!"

Memukkan had just fed Xerxes' worst fears. This had been an inside job.

CHAPTER FOURTEEN

Tears rolled down Hadassah's face as she sat down heavily on her bed in the grand suite. She remembered the way the soldiers had led her away from Mordecai towards the stagecoach that was supposed to take her to the castle.

She was dressed in a long, flowing, Persian-blue gown covered in simple, tiny pearl ornaments. She had sown it herself, investing enough time into each detail. However, her dress seemed plain next to some of the other contestants.

Remembering Mordecai's words, she pondered them. "God created you as a *unique individual* that he has set apart, inside and outside, for His glory," Mordecai had told her. "Recognize this, acknowledge it, and use it. See yourself as God sees you. Let it be the driving force behind your very existence!"

There had been a long list of demands from Mordecai. "You must go by the name of Esther now. You must remember to always answer to the name "Esther." Never forget this! You must tell no one your nationality or family background. Steer clear of unclean foods. Remain strong in the Lord and do not under any circumstances, seek out that petrifying animal."This had been Mordecai's last and final command.

Mordecai was Hadassah's biggest support system. In his eyes, Hadassah was a girl with oversized dreams and limitless potential. Would she find that same type of support at the palace?

"I'm assuming those are tears of joy!" a sassy voice interrupted Hadassah's thoughts. "I'm your roommate, Hamar, daughter of

Haman," the tall, dark-haired girl with a forced smile extended her hand--that was covered in large, gaudy gemstones--to Hadassah. Bright, bold colors popped from her eyebrows, and stiff false lashes protruded from her eyes. Her face was plastered with colored eye powders and gunk. She was tall and very gangly. But her dress was stunning! She wore a white, full gown which was fitted at the waist before it draped itself around her ankles. The sweetheart bodice was cut exceptionally low, showing far too much for a single young lady. It was covered in large, quartz stones. Although Hadassah was sure civil society would frown upon this dress, she had never seen fabric more beautiful.

"Hada..." Hadassah began to say before stopping herself. "Esther of Susa," she quickly corrected, regaining her composure even though she was still overwhelmed from being in a foreign place. She had not seen when Hamar entered the suite and made a mental note to be more alert. She shook Hamar's extended hand.

"So, you decided to take the plain road, huh?" she babbled, showing absolutely no concern for Hadassah's feelings as she dragged her extremely large trunk into the grand suite. "*Eyeliner* honey! It makes you look *alive*!" She sighed dramatically. "You'll need it, especially if you're going to be crying like that!"

Hadassah blushed, clearly embarrassed, but she did not have a chance to respond.

"Where is the help around here? I could break a nail!" Hamar exclaimed in disgust as she struggled with her load.

Hadassah got up and helped her drag the extremely heavy trunk into the suite.

"Thank you," said Hamar. She walked over to Hadassah's bed and took a seat. "I think I'll take this one. It has a view!" She smiled, sweetly at Hadassah.

Hadassah was about to protest when the door to the suite opened and in walked a man. He was middle-aged and very proficient looking. However, his presence still concerned Hadassah. Was this normal? Would strange men be in and out of their rooms? He didn't even knock to see if they were decent! He just waltzed in!

"Here we have Hamar daughter of Haman and Esther of Susa," he said, frowning down at a long scroll. He was followed by a team of fourteen servant girls all dressed in white.

"I am Hegai," he said, extending his hand towards Hamar.

"The help around here thus far has been atrocious," complained Hamar, ignoring Hegai's extended hand. "I had to carry my own trunk up fourteen flights of stairs!"

Hadassah was taken aback by Hamar's rudeness to authority. However, Hegai seemed well adjusted to insolent girls.

"Hamar, daughter of Haman," he said, bowing slightly. Hamar was about to interject when he turned suddenly towards Hadassah.

"You must be Esther of Susa." He was about to bow when Hadassah stopped him.

"There is no need for formalities," she assured him kindly. He smiled, warmly at Hadassah as he kissed her hand.

"On behalf of King Xerxes and the entire palace staff, welcome," said Hegai. He stood in the center of the suite surrounded by his team of servant girls. "I am the eunuch in charge of you girls for the duration of this pageant. If there is anything you need, just let me know, and I will do my best to accommodate you. There are one hundred and twenty-seven of you, each of you from a different province. First, we must make sure that you two are indeed virgins," said Hegai.

"W-what do you mean?" Hadassah stammered in disbelief.

"Hiding something are we?" Hamar grinned at Hadassah.

A servant, whose hands had been dipped in the ointment, escorted Hadassah to her bedchamber before drawing the curtain. Hadassah tried to relax while she let the servant girl do what she had to do.

"This is unnecessary and an absolute invasion of my privacy!" Hadassah exclaimed. She winced at the discomfort caused by the examination.

"My dear, you are in the running for the king, you no longer have privacy," responded Hegai. "I can assure you that all measures will be taken to ensure his safety and well-being."

Hadassah's palms began to sweat. She wanted to fight off the servant girl.

The servant girls both nodded in approval when they were done.

Hadassah watched as the bowls of water they dipped their hands into became muddied with red blood.

Two servant girls moved in towards Hadassah and Hamar armed with tiny saucers of a smelly green mixture. They each were told to drink the strange, green brew. It was bitter, but Hamar did not even flinch. Hadassah couldn't help but wonder if she had done this before.

"Right now, you should both be experiencing slight body aches. This is your body adjusting to the brew you have been given. The blend of herbs given will enhance your breathing. The increase in oxygen will boost your capacity to think and aid you in decision making."

Good. Hadassah thought to herself. Hamar would surely need that. She fought the urge to tell Hegai that it was probably in his best interest to give Hamar a double dose of the mixture. Hadassah had never met anyone more impolite, discourteous, and, not to mention, vulgar in all her life. She felt bad for Hegai when Hamar was rude to him.

"A special diet is planned for each of you, according to your body type and weight." He handed both of them a stone tablet, each containing an outline of their daily meals. Hadassah scanned it, happy that Mordecai had insisted that she learn how to read. Both of you have been assigned seven servant girls each. You will be provided one servant each for hair, skin, nails, speech, posture, etiquette and intelligence. There are three segments: the selection ball, the judges' interview, and your personal one-night meeting with the king."

"Oh, *a night with the king!*" Hamar gave a laugh that was somewhere between throaty and high-pitched. One could tell she was already practicing putting on airs.

An awkward silence followed.

"Ok, everyone!" Hegai broke the silence. "Let's get started. Now that we have gone over the formalities, each of you will be receiving beauty treatments." Each team of seven moved in towards Hadassah and Hamar with combs, brushes, hair serums, nail paints, oils, soaps and other beauty treatments and provisions.

"Scrub them thoroughly with sea salt, and then massage them both with oil of frankincense and myrrh," Hegai instructed the servants responsible for skincare.

Hamar screeched again in excitement. Hadassah rolled her eyes.

"Tonight, is the selection ball," announced Hegai. "There are one hundred and twenty-seven of you. Tonight, twenty-seven of you will be chosen to move on to the judges' interview segment."

He looked at Hamar. "You will each be presented with an assortment of three dresses for the selection ball tonight. You are to wear one. Choose wisely."

Across the room, Hamar had already begun barking orders at her servant girls.

"Esther," said Hegai. "Trust your judgment, and, above all things, be yourself."

Hadassah nodded. She wanted to ask Hegai why he was telling her this and not Hamar. Then again, Hamar did not seem very approachable, nor open to advice at the moment.

With those words, Hegai turned to leave. Suddenly he stopped as if remembering something. "Oh, Hamar, I see that you have chosen the bed near the window. This gives you the responsibility of reporting any suspicious behavior to the guards." With that, he was gone, leaving a furious Hamar speechless beyond words.

Hadassah stifled a laugh.

"Did you hear about the attack?" the servants whispered among themselves.

"W-what attack?" Hadassah asked quietly. Her stomach began to do somersaults.

"They don't want to scare you girls, but the palace was attacked from the inside yesterday," one of the attendants whispered. "Some say the rebels did it."

Hadassah swallowed. Her mind drifted. She could not help but wonder about Hydra. She had to find out if she was okay. While her attendants worked, she formulated a plan in her head to rescue Hydra. She did not want to disobey Mordecai, but there was something important he did not know. Hydra's eggs were hidden in the cave behind the waterfall near the ravine.

CHAPTER FIFTEEN

"I want a full report, NOW," demanded Xerxes. His nostrils flared with rage. He paced back and forth, both fists curled into tight balls.

Memukkan and the other eunuchs sat trembling, unable to find the right words to give Xerxes confirmation that the recent palace attack had been an inside job.

Xerxes tried to reel in his anger. He had allowed his temper to spill out of control once again. He had secretly sworn that he would work on this defect. These men held him in high esteem. There was no reason to instill fear into them.

"Your Highness, the attack has been fully investigated," said Memukkan. "No walls have been breached. All gatekeepers on duty have reported that there was no suspicious activity over the previous forty-eight hours prior to the attack."

"I want the army on full suspension," ordered Xerxes through gritted teeth. "No one is to leave the palace. There will be twenty-four hours of extreme, intense training. They are to partake of bread and water. NOTHING ELSE! Is that clear?"

"There is something else, Your Majesty," declaredAdmatha. "The soldiers claimed that they were affected by a sleeping herb at the time of the attack."

"Oh, really?" Xerxes mocked. "How do they know they were affected by a sleeping herb?" he asked in disgust.

"They were found groggily lying about at the time with much evidence of drowsiness. Sire, we fear that this has been an inside job," revealed Shethar.

The seven eunuchs nodded in agreement.

"Your Majesty, there is a man at the entrance, requesting that he speaks with you," a guard announced.

"Who is he?"

"It is Haman, Sire," replied the guard.

"Send him in," commanded Xerxes.

Haman entered the royal chambers. He bowed low.

"Your bravery today proved far above mediocrity, my friend," Xerxes asserted.

"It is my daily aim to serve the empire in any way I can, Your Majesty," replied Haman.

"How can I reward you for today's heroic act?" Xerxes offered. "Name your desire, and it is yours."

The seven eunuchs exchanged glances.

"I desire to serve the empire to the best of my ability, Your Highness." Haman bowed again. "This reason alone brings me before you."

"Elaborate!"

"I bring before you a written declaration," he said, placing a scroll before Xerxes. "Place your royal seal at the bottom. Give me your blessing. Make me Commander so that I may exercise VENGEANCE to its fullest capacity on our enemies."

"Are you suggesting we wage war blindly?" asked Xerxes. "WHO would we march against?"

"I am suggesting that you allow me the power to retrain the army so that we can be fully prepared whenever the enemy strikes again."

"A decision like this MUST be discussed with the council first!" interjected Memukkan.

"Memukkan is right," declared Xerxes. "Not to mention that you are running for prime minister in the next election. How will you balance both duties?"

Haman began to dramatically pace the floor.

"Tell me, Haman, what burden wears you down like this?"

"Many years ago, under the reign of your father, and before you were born, there was an attack on the palace. I was there. I witnessed incalculable acts of cruelty and unspeakable brutality. They hid behind masks and moved swiftly. I suspect that our enemy then is our enemy now. I fear they are one and the same. These monsters claimed my first wife. I seek to avenge her death and the death of the child she carried. I yearn to see to it that what happened then *never* happens again," said Haman. "You cannot hesitate, my king," continued Haman, ignoring Memukkan. "While you WASTE hours on time-consuming discussions, your enemy continues to plot and scheme. They will take away your empire and eliminate this great dynasty that you and your forefathers have built. They will be successful if we are unprepared for them."

Xerxes' eyes narrowed. The attack had angered him beyond measure. Thus far, the only person who seemed equally passionate about revenge was Haman.

"I thirst for revenge as much as you do," pleaded Haman as if reading Xerxes' mind. "It is time to settle the score."

"The times of yore are not something that we can change, Haman. However, vengeance floods my heart as much as it does yours. I approve of this declaration," pronounced Xerxes, removing his royal ring and stamping the seal on the order. "Haman will be our new battle strategist!"

The eunuchs gasped in unison.

Haman smiled widely. "You will not regret this, Your Majesty. He bowed low and then left.

Your Highness, a decision like that should have been discussed first," said Shethar.

"Your Majesty, you went outside of protocol!" exclaimed Memukkan.

The room was in an uproar.

"SILENCE!" shouted Xerxes. "He has proven himself." Xerxes narrowed his eyes. "There will be no further discussion on this matter. The seal has made my decision final. Announce to the army their new leader."

"Your Majesty, we still have another issue at hand," Memukkan informed Xerxes. "Your presence is required at the selection ball tonight."

How had he forgotten? He was so caught up with the attack that he had forgotten the selection ball! "I will be in attendance," Xerxes informed them. "Heighten security around the palace. I do not want anything to happen to the girls while they are in my care."

"Yes, Sire," said Memukkan.

"Any other updates about The Pageant?" asked Xerxes.

Shethar read from a scroll. "The girls have all been selected and are comfortably settled in the harem. They have very little or no knowledge of the attack." He paused and raised an eyebrow before carrying on. "They have all been examined to ensure that they are pure," he finished quickly.

"Very well, that sounds good. Meeting adjourned," announced Xerxes. "Memukkan, I need to see you in private please!"

"Sire?"

"You are my most trusted eunuch."

"Yes, Sire!"

"The attacker's dissection report was an interesting one," Xerxes informed him. "The cause of death was black, potent snake seeds."

"Not many people are familiar with snake seeds, Your Highness." Memukkan shifted. "They grow wild in the Southern Isles. There have been rumors of a rebellion brewing down there," said Memukkan.

"I want this investigated thoroughly," said Xerxes. "It is imperative we get to the bottom of this. Memukkan, we *must* hire a spy."

CHAPTER SIXTEEN

Susa's tall, grand buildings loomed majestically towards the sun-lit skies. The architecture of the city was beautiful. However, Hadassah was not accustomed to this kind of wealth. She stared in awe, amazed at the beauty and luxury of the city. The ride from the harem to the palace was not very long as they traveled on the streets that were lined with citizens cheering for their favorite contestant.

"It's okay to wave, Esther," said Maria from Elam.

Hadassah remained silent.

"Esther! Did you hear me?" Maria tapped Hadassah lightly on the arm. "Are you okay, Esther?"

"I'm fine," replied Hadassah, finally realizing Maria was speaking to her. *This name change will take some adjusting to*, she thought to herself.

"Well, at least smile -- you do want them to like you, don't you?" Maria prodded. "I'm practicing, starting now," and she began waving aggressively.

"You do know you're getting gold to compete?" asked Maria, still waving.

"N-N-No," Hadassah stammered.

"You will be paid one hundred gold coins just for competing." "I saw the plain dress you arrived in. You'll be able to afford many nice things after this, my dear."

Hadassah continued to look out at the shrieking fans. She didn't care about nice things, she was worried about Hydra, and it showed on her face. Where was she? How was she being treated? Was she being fed? Worry flooded her face. She tried to enjoy the parade to the palace. However, she was unable to feel anything besides worry.

Everyone except Hadassah squealed as the palace came into view up ahead. Fountains and statues surrounded the palace. The grounds were simply gorgeous.

Inside the palace was even more breathtaking. "Marble floors, dramatic candle lighting, and fourteen-karat-gold paneling!" squealed Maria. A royal staircase in the foyer lined with red velvet fabric led to a grand ballroom, which held the most amazing feast Hadassah had ever seen.

 The selection ball was like no other. The tables were laden with food for the girls. There was succulent ham soaked in pineapple and cinnamon sauce, juicy turkey, heavy with cranberry sauce, snakeskin fried as a crunchy treat, fish roasted to sublime perfection, curried goat, lobster, shelled crabs soaked in peppers, glazed conch, and chicken prepared in ways Hadassah never even imagined. Life in the palace was far from what she was used to in her village.

Her beauty team had scrubbed her generously with coconut and rose-scented sea salts. Frankincense and myrrh had been massaged deep into her skin, creating a soft, baby-like effect. Her nails were immaculately manicured, and her toes were neatly trimmed. Her team had chosen an emerald green color stain for her nails. Her perfect-color nails stunningly complemented her dress. She had chosen a deep emerald green dress that was covered in tiny jade stones. The sweetheart bodice complimented her figure to perfection. Tiny cap sleeves gracefully extended from her shoulders. Her dress, form-fitting all the way to her knees, flared around her legs, giving a charming mermaid's tail effect. Her hair was swept to the side in a way that showed off the length of her neck. A simple diamond pendant adorned her collar.

She lined up with the other contestants waiting to be presented.

"Hi, I'm Shilah of Persia," a pretty girl with dark, waist-length hair introduced herself. "This is Sia from Cush," she introduced a tall, slim girl with blonde hair and bright, blue eyes.

"Esther of Susa," replied Hadassah.

"Your dress is beautiful," they both *oohed* and *ahhed*.

"Thank you," replied Hadassah, quite distracted.

"She's so strange," Shila whispered.

Hadassah looked around the room. She tried to appear calm, but her heart was going at the speed of light. Where was Hydra being kept? Dungeons were usually underground. She would have to find a way to get to them.

"Why are there so many guards, Shilah?" whispered Hadassah.

Shilah looked a bit frightened and surprised at Hadassah's bold and unexpected question. She looked around nervously before whispering a response. "There was an attack, so the king heightened security for us." She blushed red. "That was so masculine of him!" she squealed. "He's like our knight in shining armor!"

Just then the orchestra began to play the fanfare and, at that moment, the king entered. Hadassah could not help but stare. He was handsome, no doubt. Xerxes was tall and beyond muscular; his deeply tanned skin was sunburned after hours of intense military training; his military armor added to this effect. He was polished, and the stench of charm seeped through his pores. His locks draped around his shoulders, giving him an animalistic demeanor, almost lion-like. He had a round, softly bearded face with brown, heavily lashed eyes that seemed to tell a story, his story. When the king took his seat, the procession of girls began.

Hadassah rolled her eyes as several girls began squealing like pigs. Hamar even went as far as pretending to faint. This stopped the procession for a short while as they waited for her to get up, gather her bright orange and lime dress, and finally move forward. To add to the confusion, as if her faked fainting spell wasn't enough, Hamar insisted that she stand out and march the wedding march. It was the same walk Hegai had repeatedly told her *not* to do during their practice sessions.

"HAMAR, this is a PRESENTATION feast! It is NOT a WEDDING!" he had practically shouted at her in one of the practice sessions. Hegai did not usually get angry. However, his job was important to him, and he took grooming the girls very seriously.

Hamar stupidly held her hand to her chest in a dramatic way, all the while never taking her eyes off the king. She, no doubt, wanted to be the center of attention. She began to profusely fan her face as if somehow being in Xerxes' presence caused her to lose oxygen.

Xerxes looked amused.

Hegai, who was seated next to the king, looked on in disbelief.

The audience cheered.

"She's a crowd favorite!" complained Sia, clearly stunned at being upstaged.

"Can you believe such a drama queen?" Shilah whispered loudly. "She's stealing the show!"

"Between her attire and *that* performance, she'll surely be memorable," Hadassah replied.

Shilah giggled.

"Don't worry, we're each beautiful in our own way. The king will be attracted to whomever he likes."

Hadassah was glad she was able to get Shilah to smile. Hegai had covered their teeth in camel oil just before the start of the procession.

As Hadassah walked, she studied her surroundings. The ballroom was grande beyond description. Candles and oil lamps surrounded by colored volcanic glass lined the ceiling. The table set for the girls was located directly below the king's table. She searched for an exit, but besides a powder room at the back, there was none besides the entrance they had entered when they arrived at the palace.

The orchestra's music came in loud, powerful and strong. Hadassah made a mental note to compliment them at the end of the evening. She was halfway through the procession when her glance brushed past Xerxes. Her heart nearly stopped! He was staring directly at her! Their eyes locked for a second right before he looked away. He whispered something to Hegai who nodded in agreement.

At that moment, Hadassah spotted Mordecai. She started to wave and then decided to stop. She had promised to keep their relations a secret. She smiled at him with her eyes, a sign to let him know that she was okay. He looked away without responding. Although her feelings were slightly crushed, Hadassah understood.

Hegai stood and approached the pedestal. "Ladies and gentlemen, tonight is a special night. Tonight is a night that will never be forgotten," he announced vibrantly. "Twenty-seven ladies out of one hundred and twenty-seven ladies will be selected tonight!" He paused and wiped his damp forehead with a handkerchief. "Isn't that exciting?" he asked the audience.

Whistles and shouts of approval went up throughout the crowded room. Some even started calling out the names of their favorite contestants.

"Shall we begin?" asked Hegai.

The audience gave a deafening round of applause.

"Ladies and gentlemen, we present, JOURNEY TO THE CROWN!" Hegai proudly declared as the applause continued for a few more minutes and then, finally stopped.

The orchestra launched into a slower melody as Hegai returned to his seat.

They dined and wined. Then it was time for dancing. The king watched as the girls were escorted onto the dance floor. They were paired with single bachelors from the audience who had signed up for a chance to dance with the contestant of their choice.

"At least if we don't make the cut, we'll have a chance at one of these guys," said Shilah.

"I WANT the king!" exclaimed Sia firmly.

Hadassah had never heard Sia raise her voice. She wanted to tell her that it was too early to be obsessed with winning but was rudely interrupted by a short, scrawny man with a heavy accent.

"Aye, Miss, I've been watching you!" He placed one of his hands on Hadassah's waist. "I'm Meloh."

From somewhere nearby, Hamar snickered.

"I'm going to the powder room," said Sia as a tall, stunning bachelor led Shilah away.

Hadassah began to make that her excuse as well, but before she could protest, the orchestra began to play, and the dance began.

"Ouch!" exclaimed Hadassah, after Meloh had stepped on her toes for a second time.

Meloh dragged a very reluctant and red-faced Hadassah across the dance floor.

"Are you always this vivacious?" he asked suddenly.

"What?" she gasped, trying to keep up with his atrocious dancing.

Meloh grinned widely at her, displaying a missing row of teeth.

"Lord, please help me," she silently prayed.

At that moment, a servant armed with goblets of water walked by. At that same moment, Meloh decided to spin Hadassah outward. *BRAM!*

The color drained from Hadassah's face as ice-cold water seeped down the inside of her dress. She glared at Meloh.

"I am so sorry, Miss," he said in his annoying accent. "Please let me help you!"

"You've done enough," Hadassah snapped. She turned and headed towards the powder room.

As she passed, folks began to whisper.

"Such a shame, her dress is ruined!" one whispered. "That'll take hours to dry!"

Hadassah grinned. This was the answer to her prayer. This was her chance!

CHAPTER SEVENTEEN

Xerxes stifled a yawn as the evening's festivities unfolded before him. He had put in extra hours overseeing the new training exercises of the army, and now lack of sleep was catching up with him. Despite this, however, Xerxes fought the urge. This was a very important day. He missed the company of a queen. He missed having someone to talk to. How much support could one get from a concubine? They were fun, adventurous, and pleasant to look at! However, it never went beyond that. He had learned a long time ago not to give himself away too freely. Although he immensely enjoyed the company of his concubines, Xerxes' heart was reserved for his queen alone.

When the audience began hooting again, Xerxes decided to turn his attention towards the girls.

The procession began again, and one hundred and twenty-seven girls were formally presented to the king. One, in particular, stood out from the rest. She was somewhat attractive. Each brow line was drawn to perfection, and the colors chosen were carefully dusted onto her face. Her bright orange and lime dress, though blinding to the eyes, made her assets more pronounced than her features. Hegai must have allowed them access to the royal jewelry suite because she was decked in stones of every color. Her head was adorned with a large tiara that gleamed as she approached. She had clearly made an effort tonight. That was workable. Without saying a word, she was sending a clear message. She *wanted* to be there, unlike Vashti, who never wanted to be present at his events.

The audience cheered loudly.

"Haman's daughter," said Hegai through clenched teeth.

Xerxes nodded. "Forward her to the next round," he said quietly.

Hegai, although seemingly reluctant, nodded and made his notes.

Xerxes knew that true beauty went beyond makeup and attire. However, she was the first to amuse him. After a terrible attempt at pretending to faint during the first procession, she was now fanning her face all the while keeping her eyes erotically locked on him during the entire procession.

"Look at each girl carefully, Your Majesty," said Hegai. "Choose wisely."

Xerxes nodded.

A dark-haired beauty caught his eye. She wore his favorite color, an emerald green dress covered in tiny stones that shone almost as bright as her eyes. She was slender, yet well- endowed for her size as she was curvaceous in all the right places. Though her makeup was limited, her face was *stunning*. She had full lips, and her olive skin reminded him of silk. Her lashes extended long and lengthy naturally. Her eyes caught his for a second. They were filled with depth. She did not look at him, starry-eyed like the other girls. She possessed confidence without the ego. She seemed so sure about herself. Xerxes wanted to know more about her.

Xerxes nudged Hegai. "Forward her to the next round," he signaled.

Hegai nodded. He seemed pleased. "Great choice, my king," he said in approval.

Xerxes added to the list an attractive red-head who kept giggling, along with a tall blonde who seemed a bit uptight but was pretty enough. There was also a tall ebony girl with a full head of hair that swept her waist and a sharp nose. She seemed to be preoccupied with her appearance.

"How many more do I have to choose?" asked Xerxes.

"You have to choose twenty-three more, Your Highness," replied Hegai.

Xerxes' next five picks were blondes with dark skin. He would have kept going when Hegai leaned in.

"Your Highness, is this about Vashti?" he asked intently. "Give the others a chance."

"Fine," Xerxes replied. He mixed up his remaining picks.

After the procession, dinner was served. Xerxes observed the way the girls ate and interacted with one another. Haman's daughter did very little interacting. She sat with her back exaggeratedly arched, sending a wink his way every now and again.

"Your Highness, a word," Memukkan approached him from behind.

He followed Memukkan out of the ballroom and into the courtyard.

"Your Majesty, I present the spy."

A tall, heavily bearded man bowed low. "Simeon of Cush, Sire."

"I have updated him already," said Memukkan.

"My orders are very specific," Xerxes pulled a stamped and sealed scroll from beneath his armor and handed it to Simeon. "Do your job well, and I shall reward you greatly."

"It is my honor to serve you, my king," said Simeon.

"Then go with haste," commanded Xerxes. "You have my blessing!"

Simeon mounted his horse, and in one swift motion, he was gone.

Xerxes and Memukkan returned to the ballroom.

CHAPTER EIGHTEEN

Hadassah hurried along the dark tunnels below the palace. She had managed to slip out without being seen. Thankfully, even the guards seemed engrossed in the events unfolding in the ballroom. No one was about; however, Hadassah knew that due to the recent attacks, they would be conducting more perimeter checks. She hurried along. Her heart raced in anticipation as she headed deeper into the shadowy dungeons. Hadassah's eyes watered as the stench of rotting flesh permeated the air. Yet still, she pressed on in the darkness.

"You're needed in the ballroom," said a low, gruff voice.

Hadassah jumped. She was about to answer when…

"Right away, Sir," a raspy voice answered for her.

Hadassah hid in the darkness behind the slimy wall before the guards could see her.

EE-E-K-K!

Hydra! She was alive! Hadassah's heart skipped as she silently prayed and thanked God. She peeped around the wall. There was Hydra, bound, and chained. She could barely move! She had to help her. Surrounded by several flaming torches, Hydra roared again, her nostrils flaring with smoke and flame. The guard on duty sat trembling about twenty feet away. Hadassah began formulating a plan. Deep in thought, she did not notice the shadow that had come up behind her. There was a deep nudge in her ribs before a hand was placed tightly over her mouth.

EE-E-K-K! Hydra pawed the ground ferociously.

The guard on duty looked up, startled.

Fortunately, Hadassah's muffled cries could not be heard over Hydra's roaring.

"What are you doing down here?" said a low voice. "Did I not make myself clear?"

Hadassah's pulse slowed. It was Mordecai. She hugged him tightly. "I'm sorry. I was so worried about her!"

"You could be charged with treason, Hadassah!" Mordecai scolded quietly. "This creature is forbidden!"

"This creature is my friend," replied Hadassah stubbornly.

Mordecai held his head in his hands and sat down heavily.

"So, what do you think of the pageant thus far?" asked Hadassah, trying to take his mind off her exploits. She had noticed the small gleam of satisfaction in his eye earlier and was curious to know what he thought of The Selection Ball's activities.

"Are you kidding me?" asked Mordecai in dismay. "I think that you are missing the pageant going on upstairs and should get back before someone decides to come and look for you," he growled angrily.

Hadassah stared at him. Mordecai did not get angry often. She was sorry that she had disobeyed him.

"I have to tell you something!" said Hadassah.

"What is it?"

"There are eggs!"

E-g-g-s?" spelled out, Mordecai. "Y-you m-mean l-like m-more d-d-dragles?" he stammered, suddenly barely able to get his words out.

"Yes! We have to save them!" Hadassah begged. "You have to help me!"

"Why do you care so much about this stupid creature?" Mordecai cried out angrily.

Hadassah blinked back tears. "Hydra's not stupid! She is a creation of God," she replied defensively.

Mordecai did not have a chance to respond. The sound of footsteps could be heard getting closer with each second.

"Who's there?" shouted the guard, getting to his feet.

"Relax laddie, there is no need to get excited," a deep voice thundered above Hydra's shrieking.

Hadassah gasped. It was Haman, along with a dozen guards.

"Prepare this monster to be taken to Kenswich Island in a few days," he commanded. "We leave under the cover of darkness. I want her well trained," he smirked.

"It's not possible to move a creature of this great size without being seen," said one guard.

"One can get away with anything once the right distraction is created," Haman spat onto the dungeon's floor.

EE-E-K-K! Hydra lashed out at Haman.

The other guards snickered as Haman jumped back suddenly, his eyes clouded with fear then narrowed. "If I did not need you, your head would have been on a platter by now," he cried out in disgust. Then he drew his sword as Hydra lashed out again.

Several of the guards cowered in fear behind Haman.

"Prepare four whips lined with glass, steel and the sharpest nails you can find," Haman commanded one of the guards. "I am going to break your spirit!" he sneered at Hydra.

Hadassah gasped loudly.

Haman spun around. "Who's there?" he shouted, holding his lamp out into the darkness.

"Go quickly!" Mordecai signaled Hadassah to hurry.

"I can't leave you here alone," Hadassah said stubbornly.

"Show yourself!" Haman demanded.

Mordecai held Hadassah's shoulders and looked her squarely in the eyes. "Go upstairs and do your best!" Mordecai stepped out of the shadows, revealing himself to Haman.

"It's just the Jew!" said Haman. "What are you doing down here? What are you staring at? Get back to work, *Jew!*" he sneered.

There was a resounding smack.

Hadassah knew she had to get back to the pageant. If she were caught, she would have no excuse for being down in the dungeons. If an investigation was launched, they would discover that Hydra was initially found near her home. It would not take long to figure out that she had been secretly hiding a forbidden species in her possession. Hot tears burned her eyes as she fled, leaving a brave Mordecai to take on Haman alone.

CHAPTER NINETEEN

"And rounding off our final twenty-seven is Esther of Susa," announced Hegai. He smiled and returned to his seat while the audience gave another resounding round of applause.

"She looks as if she's been crying," said Xerxes.

"Your Majesty, if I were in her shoes, I would be crying too," said Hegai. "They should all be crying tears of joy," he said as he watched Hamar stupidly bowing before the king. He shook his head as she began blowing kisses to the audience. She was smiling so wide that Hegai could have given an accurate measure of her back molars.

Xerxes took another look at Hadassah. Somehow, he could tell that her tears weren't tears of joy. She looked worried, heartbroken almost. That was a drastic change compared to her demeanor earlier. Nevertheless, he decided to take it for what Hegai said it was.

Hegai stood once again. "Now ladies and gentlemen, we present to you the interview segment!" pronounced Hegai. "Each young lady will be presented with a question. She has five minutes to answer before this happens" –– He picked up a fork and tapped it against a goblet––*DING!* He widened his eyes in excitement.

"Shilah of Persia, what do you hold most dear to your heart, and why?" Hegai asked.

Xerxes leaned in closer. This segment went beyond beauty. The interview segment displayed intelligence and each girl's ability to think on her feet. It also showed to an extent her moral fortitude and the values she stood for.

"I hold my parents' dearest to my heart," said Shilah. "They have supported me all of my life, and I am so grateful..." she stopped as her eyes welled up a bit.

The supporters for Persia began cheering before Shilah could finish.

"I am forever grateful to my parents. I love them with all of my heart," finished Shilah.

"Alright! Shilah here says that she is most grateful for her parents!" said Hegai excitedly.

It was a fair enough answer, Xerxes thought to himself. Her reply had been short and sweet. Not to mention, she expressed herself in a way that won the favor of the audience. This one showed promise.

"Now folks, we have with us Sia of Cush!" said Hegai. "Sia, what has been your biggest aspiration thus far?" he winked and grinned at the audience.

"The throne," said Sia blandly. "My biggest goal thus far has been the throne."

There was a long silence. Xerxes could hear a pin drop. It was then Sia realized her mistake. She had said the throne. She had meant to say, king. Xerxes watched as she slyly tried to correct her mistake. Even Hegai, who was never at a loss for words, seemed stunned.

DING!

"And folks, Sia's time is up!" said Hegai as he moved on to Hamar who was grinning from ear to ear.

"Hamar, what kind of queen do you believe you would make if you were chosen?" asked Hegai.

Xerxes leaned in. This question could go a number of ways. He was very interested in how this one would be answered.

"Good evening, my fellow citizens!" Hamar grinned widely as the crowd cheered in response. "First, I would support my king to the best of my ability no matter what; when he summons, I will come. Second, I would always look the part because my sense of fashion is outstanding." She cleared her throat as if her last suggestion was vital beyond measure. "Third, I would take King Xerxes to have and to hold in sickness and in health till death do us part."

The audience cheered loudly.

Fairly good answer, Xerxes thought to himself. She had given three valid points. The night drew on as each girl answered Hegai to the best of her ability. One spoke of her passion for peace, which Xerxes thought was a good answer. Another spoke of her love for her country. Xerxes thought this was noble.

"Last, we have Esther of Susa! You wear very little makeup! We want to know why?" asked Hegai. He smiled kindly at her.

Xerxes shifted. The room became silent. What a strange question! He leaned forward, anxious to hear what response would be given.

"Good evening, ladies and gentlemen," said Hadassah. Her voice was soft yet confident. "Look beyond what the naked eye can see. Hold me to the standards that lay hidden in my heart. Hold me to my standard of excellence with regard to my talents; hold me to the quality of my morals. Observe what I do in the face of adversity. Judge me by the strength I gain after a trial. Am I a victor or am I defeated when the storms of life rage around me? Do I face fear head-on or do I hide, the way some people do, behind the facial gunk and false hair?" she said. "Judge me not by my outward appearance, but by the content of my character," she finished.

There was a deafening round of applause.

The other girls looked jealously at Hadassah. It was then they realized who their competition really was.

"Why didn't Hegai ask me that question?" Hamar complained loudly. "It's not fair!"

"There you have it, folks! The end of our interview segment!" shouted Hegai above the applause.

Xerxes stared at Hadassah. He was tremendously impressed.

CHAPTER TWENTY

Hamar burst angrily into the ladies' sitting room. "You evil little twit," she said, pointing a long, angry finger at Hadassah. "You're such a spotlight hog! You didn't even answer the question!"

"What does it matter, Hamar? You're in the top five," said Shilah. "You can't always shine. Get over it!"

Hadassah had never seen Shilah so bold. "Thank you," she whispered. She smiled at her.

"Arghh!" Hamar gave a high-pitched shriek, right before flying into one of her tantrums.

The other girls ducked as feathers and fabric began flying as a result of Hamar's rage.

"If she's chosen, King Xerxes will be having another pageant very soon," Hadassah whispered.

Shilah giggled. At the back of the room, there was a table laden with treats for the girls. Shilah and Hadassah munched on freshly picked strawberries as they watched Hamar get dressed in a stunning all-white gown with a long train and veil.

The other servant girls began undressing their assigned girl. Although Hadassah felt that she would never grow accustomed to being nude in front of so many prying eyes, she allowed them to adorn her in a turquoise-blue dress lined with tiny stones. The sleeves draped lovingly over her shoulders before cascading downwards towards the nape of her back. Her servant girl swept her hair upwards high off her neck. She was presented with a pair of stunning topaz earrings, which matched her dress to excellence.

"Wow, Hadassah, your dress is so nice," complimented Shilah.

"Thank you," replied Hadassah. "Yours is lovely also!"

Shilah wore a tangerine dress that swept right below her knees. The soft angelic fabric swayed lightly with every step.

Hadassah's mind drifted to Mordecai and what had happened in the dungeons. She had spotted Mordecai in the audience sporting a smart, red mark across his cheek just before she had answered Hegai's question. She shuddered at the way Haman had told Hydra that he would break her spirit by whipping her. Hadassah knew that she was running out of time. If she wanted to save Hydra, she would have to act quickly. She would have to wait for the perfect time to sneak out.

"Esther!" Shilah's voice interrupted her thoughts. "What do you have planned for your meeting with the king?"

All eyes in the room seemed to be on her anxious to know what she would say.

"Cook," replied Hadassah.

"That's boring!" commented Hamar in a huff. "You believe that the way to a man's heart is through his stomach? Well, honey, that is a load of crap! Times are changing honey, and the way to a man's heart is through..." She struck a vulgar pose.

The other girls leaned in towards her as she lowered her voice.

"I've learned through one of Vashti's previous handmaids that Xerxes loves...." She grinned down at her audience who was now hanging onto her every word. "I plan on giving him exactly what he wants," said Hamar.

"How are you so sure that's what he'll want?" asked Hadassah.

Hamar spun around defensively. She did not like being challenged. "Xerxes and I are going to have a water get-together by the pool. What else will he want when he sees me in my swimming attire?" she dared.

Hadassah shook her head as the other girls oo*hed* and *ahhed* at Hamar's theory. As Hamar became the center of attention, Hadassah saw this as the perfect opportunity to rescue Hydra. Quickly, she grabbed a handful of tiny sardines and then quietly snuck out through the exit.

CHAPTER TWENTY-ONE

"Any word yet Memukkan?" asked Xerxes. It had been weeks since Xerxes had heard any word from the spy that he had dispatched.

"Not as yet, Your Majesty," replied Memukkan.

Xerxes sighed loudly. "I'm forced to abandon my empire while I choose a suitable wife," he grumbled. "I would much rather be hunting down my enemies. Bring in the next girl," he commanded.

The seven eunuchs had explained that the faster the pageant was over and done with, they, as a team, could focus strictly on the empire. The girls had to be taken out of harm's way as soon as possible.

"Hamar, daughter of Haman," announced Hegai. He grinned widely.

Xerxes leaned back in his chair, awaiting Hamar's entrance. He looked forward to seeing the girls, but the process was beginning to weary him. He still had a headache from the first meeting. The first girl had sung in a glass-shattering soprano voice. The second girl had struck vulgar poses the entire time. Within five minutes, Xerxes had her sent to the concubine harem. The pretty red-head had spent their entire meeting teaching him about the stars. After yawning uncontrollably several times, Xerxes finally sent her on her way. Another had been so nervous that Xerxes immediately called in Hegai to take her away. He had seen four so far, so there would be four more after them.

"Sire, for this meeting you must be escorted outside to the pools," Hegai announced.

"Oh!" exclaimed Xerxes. "This should be interesting."

"Yes, it should be," snickered Hegai.

As they approached, Xerxes could make out a flowing white gown being removed in slow motion by a tall, gangly Hamar who was there to greet him in swimming attire. She grinned at him before taking a seat beside the pool.

"Join me, Your Highness," she beckoned and then signaled a harpist, who began to play.

Hamar moved her hips in a stiff but convivial motion. Her arms flailed wildly above her head as she did a little dance before slowly settling down into the shallow end of the pool. *She certainly does get an A for effort.* Somewhat intrigued, Xerxes allowed his handmaids to strip him down to his swimming attire before joining her. He cozied down beside Hamar anxious to know what was next on the agenda.

"Tee hee, Your Highness," giggled Hamar. "You're so close!"

Xerxes gave a charming laugh.

So far, this girl was the most comfortable around him. Was she the one? He decided to dig deeper. "What are your aspirations?" he asked.

Hamar scrunched her nose. "Just stuff, you know what I mean?" She gave another high-pitched giggle.

Xerxes stared at her. It was obvious this girl was shallow. There was no depth beyond her beauty. "No, explain," he tried again.

"You know I want the best," said Hamar. "Let's just watch the moon, okay?"

This wasn't getting anywhere! "How about we go for a swim?" Xerxes asked, changing the topic. He was weary, so he decided that he may as well relax while he had the chance. He took off his bathrobe. Slowly he slipped deeper into the water. He offered a firm hand to Hamar.

"No!" said Hamar a little too loudly.

Xerxes raised his left eyebrow. "So, you're just going to sit there, huh?" he asked curiously.

Hamar glared at him. This meeting was not going the way she wanted.

"Fine, have it your way," said Xerxes. He floated away on his back while staring up at the stars. His muscles glistened under the moonlight. This pageant was beginning to prove hopeless. Maybe he was too picky, he thought to himself. Xerxes decided to try with Hamar one more time. He slowly made his way back towards the water edge where she was seated. As soon as he was close enough, he playfully splashed her.

"Are you stupid?" Hamar screamed. "What are you doing?"

"How dare you address me in such a manner?" he demanded.

Time stood still as a fuming Hamar flew into one of her famous tantrums. She became hysterical—mad beyond rage. Grabbing a towel, Hamar began frantically drying her face. Xerxes watched as Hamar's face began shifting as the gunk loosened under the pressure of the water he had splashed on her.

Everyone stared in stark horror except Hegai, who was laughing uncontrollably.

"Enough!" Xerxes shouted. "Get her out of here!"

Xerxes laid back in the pool in hopes of regaining his temper. Was he ever going to find his queen? Was he going to regain control of his empire?

CHAPTER TWENTY-TWO

"Where is the Spanish thyme?" Hadassah asked the young servant girl in a friendly voice. "It is right here, my lady," she answered, returning Hadassah's kind smile. Hadassah bustled around the kitchens in haste. She had spent the last twenty minutes preparing for her meeting with the king. The head cook had ensured her that the baby goat chosen was young and very tender. She chopped, cut, crushed and flattened before adding spices and other seasonings to her pot. There was Spanish thyme from Spain, salt from the salt ponds in the Southern Islands, and curry from Egypt. Every now and again, she tasted and scrutinized her pot.

She chopped the goat into tiny pieces. This was easy because the servants had gladly skinned it for her. They were very helpful, so Hadassah made a mental note to thank each of them as well as give them a little treat of *tostee*, which was warm bread topped with candied ginger and spiced honeyed wine.

She covered the chunks of goat in lime and sprinkled a little salt on them. She then rubbed the meat with lots of curry before placing it into the fairly large pot. "Fill this cup with water," she instructed the servant girl, who gladly obeyed. She was happy for the opportunity to learn from Hadassah and did everything with a grateful attitude. "I will add this to the pot along with those carrots, potatoes, and onions that you so nicely sliced earlier," said Hadassah. "Yes, mi' lady," the servant girl nodded, happy to be included in such an exciting process.

"Now we will mix flour and water, and roll out the bread – that will have no yeast in it," she declared, sighing happily. She was finally comfortable in this huge and foreign place even though she missed home greatly. However, cooking consoled her like nothing else.

"No yeast, mi' lady?"

"No yeast," Hadassah smiled at her. "It will be just as delicious, trust me!"

The servant girl gave an uncertain nod. She placed the flat dough Hadassah gave her into the oven.

Hadassah looked up suddenly. She could have sworn a shadow had passed across the doorway. "Get behind me," she told the servant girl as she peered into the dim lighting. There was silence. She must have thought she saw something. "Calm yourself," she told herself.

"Goat is too simple for a king," mocked a raspy voice that came from the doorway.

"Who's there?" asked Hadassah, signaling the servant girl once again to get behind her.

"You should get behind her, after all, you may be queen one day!" taunted the voice again.

"Unlike you, I'm not a coward," Hadassah replied. "Show yourself!"

Out of the shadows stepped a tall, gangly girl with messy wet hair and liquid goo that was draining around her eyes.

"Who are you?" asked Hadassah.

The girl gave a familiar sarcastic grin.

"Hamar!" exclaimed Hadassah. "Why are you poking around? You should not be here. Go away!" She continued to prepare her food all the while keeping a keen eye on Hamar, who was a very jealous girl. It was rumored that she had sabotaged some of the other girls' meetings.

"You should be serving him his favorite dish." She took a step towards Hadassah. "He loves a good ten-hour pork belly roast."

"You should be in the concubine harem," Hadassah replied coolly. She had heard about Hamar's failed *one night with the king* and knew that she was there to do whatever damage she could to destroy her meeting with the king.

Hamar looked taken aback for a moment. "I can help you know," she said with false sweetness. "I know exactly what he likes," she continued, picking up a bit of parsley before taking a step towards Hadassah.

"I do not want your help, Hamar!" Hadassah said firmly. "Take another step, and I will call the guards."

"You know nothing of royalty," said Hamar through clenched teeth. "Your clothing is simple. You wear very little jewelry. No makeup seems to please you."

"No makeup seems to please you at the moment as well," Hadassah nodded towards Hamar's own face.

"Who are you, Esther of Susa?" Hamar asked mockingly, ignoring Hadassah's comment, although her face showed that Hadassah's last comment bruised her feelings.

"Why do you ask me such questions?" asked Hadassah. "You are not the king, and you most certainly are not and never will be the queen."

As Hadassah continued cooking, the aromas rose and surrounded them with pleasant scents of spices and whiffs of Egyptian curry. The smell of freshly baked bread also inundated the kitchens.

Hamar stood there, fuming with rage. Anger began to flood her face. She was not enjoying Hadassah's defiance at all. "You can have him! He's stupid, but the crown belongs to me, not some village peasant!" Hamar screamed at her. She walked briskly towards Hadassah with a clenched fist.

Hadassah stood her ground. She opened her mouth to call out, but no sound came out.

"Hamar!"

Hamar stopped dead in her tracks. It was Hegai.

Hadassah breathed a sigh of relief.

"Remove yourself, or I will have the guards remove you."

Slowly turning around, her face overflowing with fury, Hamar stomped her way towards Hegai and out of the kitchens.

"Thank you," Hadassah mouthed to a smiling Hegai. She grinned in gratitude. "Thank you, Lord," she prayed silently.

"Now, where were we?" she said, turning towards the poor, frightened servant girl. "Shall we continue?" she smiled as she brought out the candied ginger and spiced honeyed wine.

"Yes, mi' lady," the servant girl smiled.

King Xerxes

CHAPTER TWENTY-THREE

Xerxes sat silently in the dining hall awaiting his one hundred and twenty-fifth meeting –– or it could have been the one hundred and twenty-sixth. He wasn't sure. He just wanted to get it over with. All, thus far, had failed, and now he was once again feeling hopeless. He yawned widely. The next few meetings would take place over the period of the next few days. He sighed as recollections of the last meeting with Haman's daughter, Hamar, flooded his memory. The whole thing had been a disaster, and Xerxes could not help to wonder if that was to be the worst of the bunch or if there was worst to come. He mentally prepared himself to deal with the last of the candidates. He looked down at the stone tablet Hegai had given him. "Hannah of the Southern Isles was next, and then a Shilah of Persia was to be presented the following night. Esther of Susa was to be presented the evening after Shilah."

The trumpets blared.

"I present to you Hannah of The Southern Isles."

Xerxes looked up just as a short, round, stubby girl entered the hall. She wore a bright green dress that surged upward towards her neckline and flowed outward from her waist. Its long sleeves flowed downward in such sheer excess that Xerxes wondered how she would eat her meal without spoiling her dress. As she bowed, he noticed her stomach hung over her waist.

She smiled shyly at him through her straw-colored hair that hung in short loose tendrils that framed her face.

He held out the scepter, signaling it was safe to approach.

She waddled over, and he offered her a seat at the table, and then servants began to bring out tons of food. Hannah's face lit up as servants brought out tray after tray of delectable dishes.

Xerxes could tell the idea of a large meal excited her. It was the first emotion, besides her shyness, that she had displayed all night.

There was a huge stuffed pig that was placed in the center of the table. This was followed by pig stew, crispy pig ears, roasted boar, stuffed quails, hen hot pie, meat tarts and three types of bread, barley, rye, and wheat. There were also spiced oat cake, gingered tarts, apricots, figs, prunes, currant cakes, and honeyed wine.

Hannah began to eat from her over-laden plate.

"Well, this is quite a spread we have here!" Xerxes smiled at her as he watched her waste no time, digging into the meal. She reminded him of an animal, but he just couldn't place which one.

Hannah nodded, her mouth too full to answer with words. "Pig is mi' favorite, Yer Highness," she mumbled in her thick accent. She munched loudly.

"Ah-ha," said Xerxes as if Hannah had just lit a thousand candles that brightened the entire room. It was the very animal she reminded him of. Xerxes sat and watched her for some time as she slobbered, slavered and drooled over her plate before beginning to eat from his nearly forgotten plate.

"What are your interests?" he asked after eating some of the meat tarts. The meal was fairly delicious, but Xerxes did not know if it was so delicious to the extent to cause one to fail to remember one's table manners.

"Oomph, Oomph," Hannah replied, her mouth full to the brim.

Xerxes began to look tense as he watched her chew with her mouth wide open. He gave her a friendly smile, trying not to look as uncomfortable as he felt.

"I enjoy eating, Yer Majesty," she finally said, coming up for air. She scratched her left shoulder.

"I can see that," Xerxes replied, giving her a friendly smile followed by a hearty laugh.

"What else interests you?"

"I enjoy growing mi' own food to eat," she said, beginning to stuff the pig's ears into her wide-open mouth, one by one.

"Ah!" exclaimed Xerxes as he tried to finish his meat tart, but was distracted by Hannah's awful table manners.

She scratched her shoulder again a little harder this time. She smiled, shyly at him. A piece of spinach had pressed itself across her front teeth.

Xerxes stifled a laugh. "I'm glad you're enjoying the meal," he said lightheartedly.

She smiled at him again. A loud burp escaped her lips. She looked at him with so much fear in her eyes that Xerxes reached out, touched her arm and said, "It's okay!" he said, shifting apprehensively.

"Really?" she asked in disbelief.

"Better out than in," he replied.

"That's what I always say," she said, snorting loudly. "I'm so glad I can be me self around yer," she said, farting loudly. "It feels so good not to have to hold that in any longer," she confided to him. She snorted again before noisily cleaning her teeth with her tongue. She scratched furiously.

"Are you okay?" Xerxes began to feel concerned.

Her entire face began to turn red. "I'm not sure, Yer Majesty," she said breathlessly, trying to reach down to her lower back. As she stretched, her dress began to burst open at the seams.

Xerxes looked on in horror as her swollen skin changed from red to purple. "H-Hegai!" he called out in a panic.

"I'm sorry, Yer Majesty," she apologized, and then began scratching frantically again.

"This one seems to be affected by poison oak, Hegai. This has to be sabotage."

Appalled, Hegai nodded. "I agree, Your Highness."

Xerxes felt sorry that something so unfortunate had happened to Hannah. As Hegai led her away, he made a mental note to have one of his personal servants check on her the following day.

***

The following evening…

Xerxes dug into the roasted boar drizzled with gravy. He winced as he chewed the tough but tasty meat. "Bring out the girl already," he told a tolerant Hegai who was standing patiently near the large brass doors.

"Your Highness, I do apologize, but the girl is late," said Hegai nodding politely.

"The food is going cold!" Xerxes said pointedly. "Does she not know that I am the emperor, and have the affairs of one hundred and twenty-seven provinces to attend to?"

"Yes, Your Highness, she is aware," sighed Hegai.

The trumpets blasted, and Xerxes straightened in his seat.

"Shilah of Persia," one of the soldiers announced as the brass doors were pulled apart to reveal a stunning Shilah. Her wavy waist-length hair had been pulled straight and then curled tightly to perfection. Her servant girls had pulled her hair upward in a tight bun and had let some of the curls drop in light ringlets that framed her face and neck. She was adorned in an aquamarine dress that was covered in precious stones of the same color. Her makeup was heavy but pretty, and her earrings were of the same precious stone and fell just above her shoulders. Her tiara shone brightly under the dense candlelight in the banquet hall.

Xerxes rose quickly and held out his scepter, signaling it safe for her to approach.

Shilah bowed gracefully.

Xerxes moved to the other side of the table and pulled out a chair. "Sit please do sit," he said, insisting that he assist her the best way possible.

Shilah smiled, revealing a row of pearl white teeth before sitting down.

"Wine, we need wine," Xerxes told the nearest servant. He focused his attention back on Shilah, noticing the length of her neck and how straight her back was.

"I'm sorry I am late Your Majesty," she said, smiling again.

"It is certainly no problem at all. I am all yours tonight. I usually leave my nights wide open and free whenever it is time for a meeting," said Xerxes. "I have heard that you are the perfectionist of the bunch and you are most certainly reflecting perfection tonight. I can see exactly why you are late," he chanted, ignoring the way Hegai rolled his eyes.

Shilah laughed as she accepted the goblet offered to her by the servant boy.

Xerxes chuckled. "This one seemed a bit uptight at first, but she is not afraid to loosen up," he thought happily to himself.

"You are also a reflection of perfection tonight Your Majesty." She slowly sipped the wine from the goblet. "Tell me, how does a king of your magnitude, manage to maintain such good looks and charm?" she flirted. "I imagined the king to be tight-lipped and stressed after handling the affairs of one-hundred and twenty-seven provinces," she winked.

Xerxes laughed. *She is really smooth with her tongue*, he thought to himself, deciding to turn on his charm.

"Imagine my delight when I discovered otherwise," she purred. She took another sip of wine all the while never taking her eyes off of him.

"How about a toast?" asked Xerxes.

"What shall we toast to?" Shilah asked sweetly.

"Happiness," smiled Xerxes.

"To happiness and meaningful, long-lasting friendships," added Shilah, before gulping down the rich red wine. She swallowed and placed her goblet near the golden plate. "Well quite a spread we've got here, have we?"

"What would you like to eat?" asked Xerxes.

"Is that roasted boar?" Shilah asked. "My favorite! How did you know?"

"Roasted boar it is," said Xerxes signaling for the servants to fill Shilah's plate with whatever her heart's desire.

"What is your favorite, Your Majesty?"

"I love a good tender lamb or goat prepared to perfection."

"Guess what?" Shilah whispered.

"What?" Xerxes whispered back.

"That is my second favorite," she said in a low voice.

"My second favorite is roasted boar with mint jelly," said Xerxes in an even lower voice.

"Why are we whispering?" she whispered, smiling.

"You started it!" said Xerxes. They both burst out laughing.

"Have you ever tried those exotic meats that they serve in the bazaar?" Shilah asked. "They're quite the rave you know."

"Are they?" Xerxes turned spontaneously to the servant beside him. "Bring out the snake eyeballs," he said. He winked at a giggling Shilah.

"You naughty…" she wagged her finger at him before she began to sip from the golden goblet once again.

"So, this is what a king eats," Shilah sighed. "I have always wondered."

Xerxes smiled at her innocence.

The servants brought out two bowls laden with snake eyeballs and gravy.

Shilah clapped her hands in excitement. "You first!" she laughed.

"Let's do it together on the count of three," said Xerxes.

"Great idea!" said Shilah, spooning up an eyeball. She watched as Xerxes fished up the smallest eyeball in his bowl onto the spoon.

She rolled her eyes and laughed. "Ok fine!"

"One…two…three." They both giggled as they spooned the snake eyeballs into their mouths.

"Such an odd flavor!" Shilah laughed hysterically.

Xerxes winced. "It's so slimy!"

"The look on your face is hilarious!" Shilah laughed again before spooning another slowly into her mouth and chewed. "May I ask a question, Your Highness?" She drank from the wine goblet once again.

"You may ask whatever your heart's desire," said Xerxes finally picking up his forgotten chalice for the first time.

"Why do you raise taxes?" she asked curiously. "It aggravates the rich and makes them bitter, and it is beyond taxing on the poor. No one is happy after paying taxes. Shouldn't your people be happy?"

Xerxes leaned back in his seat, not sure if he felt like discussing politics after having such an enjoyable time with this obviously spontaneous girl. He loved her bold and free spirit. "Taxation has always been the system put in place in order to raise money for royal expenses."

"Expenses?" Shilah repeated slowly.

"There are great things on the royal agenda for this upcoming year."

"Really!" Shilah said, lighting up. She took another drink of wine. "This wine really carries down this snake soup well."

"It wasn't so bad. The flavors are growing on me," he said. "Are you okay?" he asked, noticing the way Shilah began to hold her head as if in pain.

"Yes! Of course! I am fine!" she assured him. "So, can I see?"

"See what?" asked Xerxes.

"The royal agenda, of course!" she said.

"Oh sure," said Xerxes with a little less certainty than before. "I don't see any harm in that."

He got up, slid his chair back slowly. "I just need to arrange my cloak and a cape for you, and we shall be on our way."

"Why do we need cloaks and capes," she asked fanning herself. "It's hot in here."

"We must walk through the gardens to get there. It is a bit windy out." He turned toward the servant. "Fetch Hegai and a cloak for myself and the lady."

Shilah smiled at him. She seemed in a daze, and Xerxes could tell she was trying to remain upbeat.

"Tired, are we?" he asked.

She smiled again.

"I brought the cloaks, Your Majesty. We're in for a small bit of cool breeze tonight," said Hegai as he first assisted Xerxes with wrapping the cloak in a way that ensured the king would be protected.

Suddenly Hegai's mouth dropped open. He speechlessly tapped Xerxes on the arm and signaled to him to turn around.

Xerxes turned slowly. His heart sank. There lay Shilah, fast asleep, face-down in the snake soup. It was just as he had feared. She was drunk.

CHAPTER TWENTY-FOUR

Xerxes sat in the great dining hall awaiting the last and final contestant. He was weary with disappointment. Every meeting had proven unworthy of his standards. *Maybe my standards are too high*, he thought to himself. His father had taught him to never relax his standards, for the requirements of a king determined the kind of king he would be. He missed his father dearly. However, he was grateful for the time they had spent together. He had learned much from him. However, he always felt that there was more to learn if he intended to excel.

The trumpets blared announcing the arrival of the last and final contestant.

"Next, we have Esther of Susa," Hegai announced enthusiastically.

Hadassah entered the magnificent dining hall with forced composure. Although surrounded by gold paneling, thick silk curtains, and rich Persian rugs, she still felt depressed amidst all the luxury. She tried to take her mind off Hydra just for the night. But was this really important? Should becoming queen really be that much of a priority when a friend was in trouble? True, there were laws against dragles, but if one got to know them, one would discover that they were very gentle and intelligent creatures.

Xerxes looked up. Standing before him was the beautiful, young lady whom he thought had been crying. He held out his scepter as a sign for her to approach. However, she just stood there, eyes cast downward and seemingly deep in thought.

"Are you afraid of me?"

The king's words interrupted her thoughts, bringing her crashing back to reality. "No, Your Highness!" She signaled to the servants to begin bringing in the meal she had prepared earlier. Hamar had laughed at her and told her that goat was too simple for a king. Hadassah had prepared her meal of spicy, curried goat and unleavened bread with love, all the while ignoring Hamar's jeering and sneering. She scrunched her nose as she remembered Hamar's ten-hour pork belly roast suggestion. Pork was considered unclean, and Hadassah being a Jew could not touch it, let alone eat it.

"What's wrong?" he asked.

"A thought struck me, Your Majesty," she said, taking the seat he offered her at the table.

"Do you care to share?" he asked.

"My fellow contestant, Hamar, had suggested I serve a ten-hour roast to you!" She looked at him as the servants plated their meal. He was watching her very carefully. He was careful not to show the slightest emotion the way kings were trained to do.

Her heart nearly stopped as he took the golden fork and advanced towards his plate. "You're doing it wrong, Your Majesty," she stopped him.

"Oh?" he replied.

Hadassah tore a piece of unleavened bread with her fingers and dipped it into the curried goat mixture, trapping some of the goat and the gravy between the bread.

"May I?" she asked, holding it inches from his mouth as she beamed at him. "This is how it is meant to be eaten."

Her nerves calmed a bit as Xerxes leaned in and gently took the food from her fingers and placed it into his mouth. Her heart praised God as his face softened.

"This is ten times better than any ten-hour roast I have ever had," declared Xerxes.

Hadassah beamed at him.

"Didn't Hegai give you all one hour to prepare?" he asked curiously.

Hadassah nodded, stifling a giggle.

"A ten-hour roast would have been a terrible idea!" he exclaimed as he reached down and began to eat his meal the way Hadassah had just shown him.

"Exactly!" she laughed aloud, digging into her own meal.

They dined in silence for the next few minutes. Hadassah watched as he savored every bite. She felt proud. Every moment in the kitchens back at the humble cottage she shared with cousin Mordecai had prepared her for this very day.

"I did not know bread without leaven could be just as good," said Xerxes, his mouth full. He turned to the servant who was now pouring the wine. "Please send my compliments to the cook. He did an excellent job here today."

"You can give regards to the cook yourself, Your Majesty," the said Hegai. "Esther prepared this meal."

"Oh?"

She beamed again wanting to laugh at the stunned look on the king's face.

"You possess great talent," said Xerxes, getting up and bowing.

"Please Your Highness, there is no need to bow to…" her voice trailed off as his heavily lashed eyes met hers. She could not help noticing how handsome he was. His locks had flecks of gold running through them, and his muscles were firm and unyielding.

Xerxes sat back down, his eyes fixated on her. He reached for his food again. "Ouch!" he exclaimed as he quickly yanked his arm back.

"What's wrong?" Hadassah asked, her heart sinking.

"The knife nicked me."

Hadassah rushed over to examine it. "Bring me some aloe," she said to the servant. She was so accustomed to taking care of Mordecai that this came naturally to her.

"Really, it's only just a scrape," Xerxes said.

"Still, it should be treated to prevent infection," Hadassah insisted just as the servant returned. "Please stay still," she said. The servant had returned with a bit of crushed aloe. Hadassah gently applied just the right amount to his forearm. "The aloe seals over the cut and prevents infection," she said.

"Why do I get the feeling that you're good at this?" Xerxes beamed at her. "How is it you know all of this?"

"Before I came here, I used to take care of my cousin." She smiled up at him. "He was rather clumsy."

"Are you calling me clumsy?" he asked, smiling sheepishly.

"I don't think you're clumsy," Hadassah beamed again. "In fact, I think that this little accident was intentional."

"Oh?"

"Because now I will have to feed you," Hadassah said as she reached for his meal. She tore the unleavened bread once again with her fingers and dipped it into the curried goat. "Tonight, I cater to you, my king," she said softly. As she brought the meal to his mouth, she could not help noticing how full his lips were. She blushed as he once again fixed his eyes on her.

"Who will take care of you?" he asked softly, interrupting her thoughts. He leaned in and kissed her. Hadassah's head swam. She could not believe that this was happening to her. Butterflies rose in her stomach as he looked lovingly at her before rising and bringing her to her feet and kissing her again, more deeply this time.

Hadassah wondered if he was thinking straight. She wondered if she was even thinking straight. She had just had her first kiss ever.

"What do you mean?" she asked breathlessly.

"In my royal chamber," he said, stopping and looking at her longingly.

"Your Majesty I..." Hadassah's voice caught in her throat before trailing off.

"What's wrong?" asked Xerxes. "Out of one hundred and twenty-seven girls, I feel most connected to you," he said softly. "Please afford me the honor."

Hadassah shook her head and said, "No, I cannot do that!" She trembled at the thought of her fate. To anger, a king was a terrible act that came with terrible consequences. She looked up at him, her eyes filled with pure love.

"You would deny a king his greatest desire?" asked Xerxes.

Hadassah slowly took a breath. How does one explain to a king that his desires cannot be granted due to one's personal beliefs? She prayed silently before answering him.

"I have been waiting all my life to share myself with my husband and my husband alone. If I lie with you tonight, I am your concubine and nothing more!"

"But I want what I feel to flower into something that's real and true and pure," said Xerxes.

Hadassah shook her head once again. "True love honors another's purest beliefs. I beg you, my king, do not force me to break my vow to myself and, more importantly, to my God."

"This is hard for me," he said, clearly frustrated. "But I will honor your belief, my dearest Esther."

In relief, Hadassah exhaled slowly. She had not realized until then that she had been holding her breath.

"You are free to go," said Xerxes. He looked after her as she fled the room. He was sure he had noticed her eyes welling up with tears, yet, he wasn't sure. Any of the previous one hundred and twenty-six girls would have given themselves away to him in a heartbeat, and yet, she had turned him down. She had turned down a king! However, Hadassah had given him a lot to think about. He made his way to his bedchamber—alone.

As Hadassah ran from the room, hot tears began to spring from her eyes. "Did I anger him? Do I still have a chance?" she thought to herself. Racing to her chambers as fast as her legs would take her, she collapsed onto her bed. Her shoulders shook with sobs.

"I told you he was stupid," Hamar's voice said quietly.

They must not have taken her to the concubine's harem yet, Hadassah thought. Ignoring her, Hadassah rolled over and quietly cried herself to sleep.

CHAPTER TWENTY-FIVE

The bland, stony walls of the drippy, dark dungeons thrust themselves upward, spiraling towards an endless abyss Hadassah could not see. Yet, she pressed onward towards Hydra's screams, all the while battling the fear that surged within her. What if she were caught? How much time did she have? She was no longer concerned about what had transpired on her date with the king. Her only concern was to see her friend to safety. She shuddered at what the whip, Haman had ordered to be created for Hydra, could do to her. Her eyes narrowed and her teeth clenched at the thought of Hydra's perfect white flesh being ripped to shreds by glass, stone and metal, all for Haman's pleasure. She could not allow it. Haman was the real monster. She would find a way to make him pay.

"Upstairs!" a guard shouted.

Several guards ran towards Hadassah just before she ducked behind the slimy wall of the dungeon. One, two, ten, and thirteen—Hadassah counted as they ran past her hiding place. Hadassah couldn't help but wonder if this sudden chaos had anything to do with the distraction Haman had mentioned many days earlier. It was then she realized how much in the dark she was with regards to Haman's plan. Her own plan was to wing it! However, she could only hope her spontaneous act was enough to save Hydra.

EE-E-K-K!

Hadassah peeped from behind the dungeon's wall.

There Hydra loomed, no longer chained. She was surrounded by tons of hay, and a single rope held her firmly, deterring any thought of escape that might enter her mind. Hay! Really, would a water dragle eat hay? Hydra must be starving! The rope was tightly knotted and attached to a catch somewhere in the ground. Good. Hadassah did not know about chains but a rope she could handle. Loosening the noose of her dress and removing a few sardines, she threw them towards Hydra who hungrily devoured them. Crouching low on her tummy, she inched towards Hydra.

Hydra must have sensed her. She viciously pawed the ground. Her nostrils flared with smoke and fiery brimstone.

Thankfully Hydra was alone. Not a guard was in sight. As she got closer, Hadassah studied her closely. Besides a few cuts around her neck area, she seemed fine. Hadassah breathed a sigh of relief. Haman must not have had the chance to whip her as he had planned.

EE-E-K-K!

"Shhh," Hadassah cooed, trying to calm her down. Hadassah moved silently along towards Hydra, well shaded by the shadows of the dungeon's walls. Just a few more inches and she would be able to reach the rope and free her entrapped friend. "Two more inches and…"

The sound of footsteps could be heard getting closer and closer to her. Instinct told her that within seconds, the dungeon would be flooded with soldiers armed with whips and chains, ready to cart Hydra off to Kenswich Island in the Southern Isles. She had to move swiftly. Careful to remain hidden in the hay, Hadassah went to work maneuvering the knot.

"We've ten minutes, starting now!" one guard shouted.

"Chain her!" another prodded loudly.

The dungeon was filling up with guards fast, and soon they would be surrounded by them. Ignoring the fear that surged within her, Hadassah continued to manipulate the knot as guards closed in on them. She remained hidden.

Another tug and a pull, and finally, the knot came free! The sudden force of freedom knocked Hydra sideways sending her into a fit of vigorous rage. "Uh-oh," Hadassah exclaimed softly. The rope that was now free launched into the air, wrapping itself around the powerful muscles of Hydra's neck. The more she fought, the tighter the rope became preventing oxygen from flowing freely into the magnificent animal. Hydra's eyes gleamed in wild fear.

A lump rose in the back of Hadassah's throat. "Shhh, it's going to be okay," whispered Hadassah on the verge of tears. Her body shook hysterically as she reached forward and placed one hand on Hydra. Within seconds she felt Hydra relax under the familiar weight of her hand. She needed to get onto Hydra's back in order to remove the rope. Hadassah prayed that Hydra would keep her wings extended, giving her enough time to climb onto her back without being seen.

The guards were shouting and scurrying into place so that they could put the chains on Hydra.

Another knee up and she would be firmly seated. Hadassah held on tightly as she inched her way towards the noose of the rope. There was a scuffle with the loop, and then suddenly it fell away.

Hadassah held on for dear life as Hydra viciously pawed the ground. They were surrounded. How would they get out of this? Determined not to leave Hydra alone, Hadassah searched for an escape route.

"She's broken the rope!" an out of breath guard shouted in dismay.

"She's going to escape!"

Hadassah's eyes widened as another guard tore out a whip. He brought it down heavily on Hydra's gleaming white side, tearing away flesh and bone.

Suddenly struck with the terror of ferocious pain, Hydra's eyes seethed with anger, and as she violently fought, her foot struck something hard.

Water poured in from below. Hydra must have burst a conduit of some sort. The dungeon was filling up with water fast. If they didn't get out, they would surely drown.

Hydra breathed down hails of fire and brimstone upon the guards below. The dark dungeon was now a firestorm as smoke and flames blazed violently. Still, the guards armed with chains continued to press towards Hydra anxious to make her their captive again.

Hadassah looked upward as she silently prayed for help. It was then that she noticed a tiny star glistening in the distance. The dungeon's walls must lead to an opening of some sort. This was the way out. Expertly digging her heels into Hydra's side, she prepared her to jump.

"LEAP!" she whispered loudly. Together they climbed upwards towards the heavens, leaving behind the chaos—leaving behind the pandemonium—they flew upwards towards freedom.

CHAPTER TWENTY-SIX

Xerxes' heart plummeted as shouts and screams echoed throughout the palace. Still drenched with anger, he pummeled through the castle's walls, thirsty for revenge.

"Your Majesty, you must at least put on your armor!" Memukkan shouted. He was thankful when Xerxes took heed, and rushed to his chamber, obeying right away. He helped Xerxes gear up and then handed him his bow and arrow.

"Be safe Your Highness," he said, patting him on the shoulder.

"Thank you, Memukkan," said Xerxes. "Now off to the safe room you go!" he insisted kindly.

Memukkan looked at Xerxes in confusion. In return, he saw genuine gratitude. He had noticed a change in him over the past few weeks. Xerxes was beginning to change. In Xerxes' eyes, he saw a friend. Instead of scurrying away to safety, Memukkan picked up a sword of his own. Just then Shethar, Tarshish, Meres, Carshena, Admatha, and Marsena entered with their swords.

Memukkan smiled. "Together, we will fight to save this empire," he declared with forced confidence. "Par Eunephia: For Prosperity!"

Xerxes was proud of his eunuchs. He was not alone. "For Prosperity!" Xerxes echoed loudly.

Together they pressed into the shadows against the walls of the palace.

All was still.

"Do you guys hear anything?" Xerxes whispered.

"Just Memukkan's teeth were chattering," Shethar joked.

"Ouch!" Shethar yelled as Memukkan brought his foot heavily down on his toe.

"You didn't have to…"

Xerxes covered Shethar's mouth tightly. He signaled for the others to be quiet just as a dark shadow flew past the corridor. The corridor led to a wide balcony that protruded over a cliff and extended over stormy waters. Xerxes signaled again to the seven eunuchs to follow the assailant onto the balcony.

A resounding crash could be heard, and something landed on the balcony.

"What is it?" asked Meres.

"It is a warning!" Memukkan's eyes widened as he peeled away the black cloth to reveal a single sword with the engraving, 'Simeon' on it. His head hung in grief.

Memukkan and Xerxes exchanged knowing glances.

EE-E-K-K!

"We need to split up and look for the attacker!" Xerxes shouted.

No one obeyed. The seven eunuchs seemed glued to the ground.

Memukkan's mouth hung open in awe. "D-D-d-d…" he stammered.

Xerxes rolled his eyes. "Spit it out already!"

Xerxes' eyes followed Admatha's extended finger towards the skies. "Dr-Dr-Dragle!" he screamed.

Xerxes looked up in stark horror. Squinting, he could just make out the fire-breathing creature. It was who was on the back of the dragle that stunned him. It was a familiar young girl waving her arms frantically, as if in a warning. She pointed behind him. He turned in time to see an attacker, all in black, flying towards him at top speed. The wide-open balcony loomed ahead. The only safe path to take, without hurting his eunuchs, was straight ahead towards the cliff. Xerxes began to run forward. He looked back. The attacker was close behind. He had no choice. He would have to jump!

The treacherous water thrashed below. Jagged rocks and limestone jutted upwards, threatening any who dared grace their presence. Xerxes leaped up and turned suddenly in mid-air, unsheathing his bow and arrow and successfully placing an arrow directly into the heart of his attacker. Within that same second, he turned upwards and aimed for one of the dragle's hind legs.

"A king never misses his mark," he whispered.

EE-E-K-K!

Down went Xerxes. Down went the attacker. Down went Hydra. Down went Hadassah.

CHAPTER TWENTY-SEVEN

Pain surged through Hadassah's cold, frail body. Her eyes blinked open. She sat up, panicking. Where was Hydra? Was she alive? A grand metal contraption filled with hundreds of tiny candles extended from the ceiling above the soft bed. The bright-red silk bedding was embroidered with gold detailing, like the sun. Two matching chairs of the same fabric stood in the corner. Seated in one of them was Hegai.

Hegai's brows were furrowed deep in thought. "I have been waiting for you to wake up," he said glumly.

Hadassah burrowed deeper into the thick warm blankets. The horrific events of the previous night replayed over and over in her head like a scorching record.

"My dear," said Hegai, coming closer to the bed. "You have been summoned."

"Me?" said Hadassah, her voice barely above a whisper. Of course, she would be summoned after what had happened. She could only imagine how furious the king was going to be. A dragle was a forbidden species, and she was seen riding one. What would her fate be? Her eyes widened at the thought of being beheaded. Her shoulders slumped in defeat. She had brought shame to Mordecai.

"Is Hydra okay?"

"Hydra?" Hegai's expression went from solemn to one of confusion.

The door opened.

"The king is ready to proceed," a guard announced.

Hegai nodded.

Painfully, Hadassah got up and allowed Hegai to help her into a loose-fitting emerald green gown. He combed her long thick tresses downward, and then he spiraled them outward into thick, wavy, waist-length bouncy curls. She allowed him to dab a little red lip stain onto her lips. Around her neck, he placed a single simple pendant.

"There," said Hegai. "You look presentable!"

Hadassah was led up one corridor and down another until they finally arrived at two bronze doors. Two guards pulled them apart to reveal a single throne on which Xerxes sat. Hadassah tried to ignore the way she trembled at the sight of him. Her heart sped at a speed that was immensely uncomfortable. Tears threatened as she imagined what the next few moments held for her. It was rumored that when death came swiftly, one didn't feel the pain associated with it.

"Esther of Susa," announced the guard.

Xerxes held out his gold scepter towards her.

Hadassah reached out, just enough to acknowledge the scepter. She was too afraid to look into Xerxes' eyes.

Reading from a scroll, the guard announced, "Esther of Susa, you have been found guilty of the following: "Endangerment of King Xerxes, Endangerment of Palace Domain and Association with a Forbidden Species." The guard rolled the scroll up. "How do you plead?"

"G-gu-guilt…" Hadassah's lips barely moved above a whisper.

"NOT GUILTY!" answered Xerxes.

Hadassah looked up, confused. Xerxes, who was now smiling at her, got up from his throne and walked towards her.

Had he gone mad? What was going on?

"My dear, your bravery, and beauty have greatly impacted me," he said, watching her with gratitude. "You deserve the great things that are coming to you!"

"What do you mean?" Hadassah stammered in bewilderment.

Xerxes slowly moved in toward her. "I've wanted you from the moment I laid eyes on you, Esther. Never have I beheld such rare beauty in a woman inside and out. I want to be in your arms, encircling your heart with kisses, caressing you with the best of me. I want to crawl into your empty spaces, filling your life with pure love, marching my way into the battlefield of your heart, declaring war on all those who hurt you, and conquering each pain with firm strokes of my sword!" For the first time in a long time, Xerxes smiled. "I yearn to know you better."

"My Dearest Esther," he said. "I choose you! You have been...*chosen!*"

MESSAGE FOR TODAY

Dear Reader, the story of Hadassah tells of how God can take an exiled individual and use them as his vessel despite their background, nationality, and their heritage. It shows that God is the overall regulator who is in complete control no matter how bad circumstances may seem. He can take an exiled girl from rags to riches. He places crowns on the heads of slaves. He is so powerful that he can save a nation through a single orphaned girl.

Romans 10:9 New International Version (NIV) tells us that "If you declare with your mouth, "Jesus is Lord," and believe in your heart that God raised him from the dead, you will be saved.

Here is a simple prayer if you have not yet given your life to Jesus and invited him into yours:

Jesus, I believe you are the Son of God, that you died on the cross to rescue me from sin and death and to restore me to the Father. I choose now to repent of my sins and every part of my life that does not please you, and I accept you as my personal Lord and Savior. I choose you. I give myself to you. I receive your forgiveness and ask you to take your rightful place in my life as my Savior and Lord. Come reign in my heart, fill me with your love and your life, and help me to become a person who is truly loving—a person like you. Restore me, Jesus. Live in me. Love through me. Thank you for saving me. I place my full dependence on you, and I ask your complete guidance in my life. In Jesus' name, I pray. Amen.

Congratulations and welcome to the family of the one true King! The angels are rejoicing in the spiritual realm because you have been adopted into the family of God. You are now his son/daughter. Wear your spiritual crown daily. Live out your purpose through your God-given talents and remember that you are a fisher of men for his kingdom! The task ahead of you will not be easy. Satan will assign demons with special assignments to distract and discourage you from your true purpose, which is to be a soldier for the army of Christ. Babylon, Medo-Persia, Greece, and Rome have all risen and fallen like the Lord revealed to King Nebuchadnezzar. The first part of King Nebuchadnezzar's dream has unfolded, just as God revealed to Daniel. Why should we doubt the second part of it? The part yet to be unfolded is the stone smashing the statue to pieces. My friend, the next great event is the coming of Christ. I urge you to be ready. I encourage you to live for Christ daily.

Book 2 in the Silent Soldier Series-Blood, Sweat and Tears (Coming Soon)